The Friends of the
Lansdowne Public Library
Book-a-Year-Forever

In honor of

Ruth Dote

The Lipstick
Killers

www.noexit.co.uk

Other titles by the author

Gangsters Wives

THE LIPSTICK KILLERS

KILLERS

LEE MARTIN

NO EXIT PRESS

First published in 2009 by No Exit Press,
PO Box 394, Harpenden, Herts, AL5 1XJ
www.noexit.co.uk

A CIP catalogue record for this book is available from the British Library.

ISBN 978-1-84243-260-0 (Hardcover)
ISBN 978-1-84243-261-7 (Trade paperback)

2 4 6 8 10 9 7 5 3 1

Typeset by Avocet Typeset, Chilton, Aylesbury, Bucks
Printed and bound in Great Britain by JH Haynes Ltd, Yeovil, Somerset

For Kesh

PROLOGUE

August Bank Holiday Monday 1989. Party time at the Doyles and everyone was showing their best faces. Roxanne – Roxie for short – Doyle's sixth birthday. Named after her father Mickey's favourite Police song, she was. The spoilt baby in the family of four daughters. Frances known as Frankie, the eldest at thirteen. The clever one. University material, everyone said. Then Margaret – who would only answer to Mags. Eleven-years-old. Crazy like a fox. Smart too, but already showing a resentful streak when it came to authority. Next, Sharon. Nine. Sweet, but docile enough to be easily led into bad ways. And finally of course Roxie. The baby – the apple of everyone's eye, especially their mother.

'Five bleedin' women,' their dad used to say. 'Five in one house, and just me to get stick day and night. I can't get away with anything.' The sisters fought each other like cats and dogs, or more like cats and bitches, but beware of any outsider sticking his or her oar in. Then they become one. A four-headed Hydra looking for a ruck. The bigger the better. Like when one of the bigger boys at school cut the end of Sharon's plait one day, then was ambushed on the way home by the girls – four-year-old Roxie being let loose on his head with a pair of scissors whilst Frankie and Mags held him down. He looked like he had alopecia when she finished, and she always swore that it was that day she decided her later choice of career as a hairdresser.

Their dad complained, but he didn't mean it. They knew as well as him that he was secretly proud of his feisty brood. And the mock-Tudor mansion in Streatham, south London was big enough for him to get lost in if needed. From the playroom in the attic, down five floors to the basement where there was a juke box, wet bar, pool table, and the biggest colour TV currently available linked into a state-of-the-art video recorder and music centre, plus a vast collection of films, records and tapes. Or in the five car garage at the side of the house which held Mickey's collection of vintage cars and top of the range Harleys.

That boiling hot Monday though, all the action was outside in the back garden that stretched four hundred yards to a bank of trees that hid the South Circular road from view. A wooden floored marquee had been erected for the finest food and drink money could buy. Moet flowing like water. Nouvelle cuisine for the adults, and burgers and fries for the kids. A DJ had set up twin decks to play the hits of the day by Kylie, Jason, Madonna, The Bangles for the kids, but with plenty of golden oldies for the grown-ups when the dancing and boozing really got going after sunset. Sure it was loud, yeah. But fuck it, it wasn't everyday, and besides the neighbours had been invited. If they chose not to come, well let them close their windows and doors and watch bloody *Eastenders*. They wouldn't complain. At least not to the face of the lady of the house, Queenie Doyle. Real name Alice, which she detested. She christened herself Queenie at an early age, and the way she ran the south London scene like a monarch, it fitted perfectly. She scared the shit out of them, as did her daughters. The neighbours called them the Wild Bunch, despite seeing them in their private school uniform every day. They lowered the tone of the area, said the school playground gossip. Must be incomers from Catford or Lewisham or some such. Too much money and not enough manners they said – as long as Queenie or one of her clan couldn't overhear them.

Queenie didn't care what those snobby bitches at the school gates said. She had family all over south London. No fucker messed with the Doyles. The house was theirs, bought and paid for. No mortgage. And cash was rolling in from all directions. Too much sometimes. So let's have some fun, spend some dough. It's party time, and that was all that mattered – for now.

By three pm the place was buzzing. The private road the Doyles lived in was rammed with cars. Rolls-Royces, Bentleys, Aston-Martins, Ferraris, Cadillacs, Porsches, all shiny and new. A million quids' worth of motors by anyone's reckoning. The lounge was so full of toys for Roxie that Hamleys' shelves must have been empty. Wrapping paper and cards littered the floor as she ripped open the parcels delivered by friends and family. Outside the disco was booming and the sisters were practising their dance routines with the few friends from school they'd invited. Not many. The Doyle girls didn't pal up easily. They didn't need to – they had each other.

The front door was open wide to allow easy entry for the guests. They came in all shapes, sizes, colours and sexual inclinations. Say one thing for the Doyles, they played no favourites. Queenie was the boss, and Queenie knew that it took all sorts. And they all had their uses. Whores, pimps, drug dealers, gangsters of every stripe, bookies, even some coppers who were on the payroll. It was a family day and all were welcome to eat, drink and have a laugh at the Doyles' expense. No trouble. That was the only rule, and a half-dozen or so heavy looking individuals were scattered around the place front and back, to make sure that everyone stuck to that particular rule – sweating in their dark suits to disguise whatever weapon of choice sat beneath.

Despite the heat Queenie felt cold and wore a mink wrap around her shoulders. She put down her champagne glass and excused herself and went upstairs to her and Mickey's bedroom, and went into the en-suite. She dropped the stole onto the floor and stripped off her dress and bra. The lumps were still there under the skin of her ample breasts. She was the only one who knew. She hadn't let Mickey touch her for months, maybe a year. More lumps than she remembered, and they were tender to her touch, sending pain down to her crotch. She knew she should go to the doctor, but she had no time for them. The pain made her vomit into the toilet and she cried as she knelt on the floor. 'Oh, girls,' she said to herself. 'I'm so sorry.'

1

———❖———

A ringing phone in the middle of the night always brings life-changing news. News of a death, or a birth. And so it was when Margaret Doyle was woken from a restless sleep at three in the morning. She didn't yet know it, but she woke to a day that would change her life and that of her family forever. She fumbled for the receiver in the dark, and the empty wine glass on her bedside table bounced onto the carpet. 'Shit,' she mumbled, then spoke into the phone. 'What?'

'Mags, it's me,' said the voice on the other end of the line.

'I know who it is,' said Margaret, her voice full of sleep. 'What do you want at this time of night?'

'It's Monty,' said the familiar female voice. 'He's dead.'

Margaret tried to pull herself awake through the fog of alcohol and the sleeping pill she'd taken at midnight. 'Do what?'

'Monty. Our brother-in-law. Sharon's husband – he's dead.'

Margaret sat up, switched on the bedside lamp, winced at the light, then said, 'wait a minute Frankie. Just wait.' There was a bottle of Evian water next to the lamp, and she put the receiver under her chin and grabbed it, unscrewed the top and took a long drink. 'That's better,' she said. 'Now what are you talking about?'

'Listen,' said Frances Foster, nee Doyle. 'Monty's dead. Have you got that?'

'This is no joke?'

'For fuck's sake Mags. I'm not in the habit of making jokes at this time of night,' snapped her sister.

Or any other time, thought Margaret, but said nothing. She checked the bedside clock. 3.14 a.m. 'He was coming home from some do or other in Southampton,' Frankie went on, 'it was pissing down with rain and the car came off the road near Petersfield. It hit a tree. He was killed outright they reckon.'

'Who reckons?' said Mags, immediately switching to business mode. In her job, she was used to matters of life and death.

'The doctors here, and the cops.'

'Where's here?' asked Margaret.

'Guildford Hospital. I'm outside in the rain having a fag. I can't stand it in there.'

'Was he pissed?'

'Trust you to ask that. Always the copper.'

'Well, was he?'

'I don't know. He could've been. Out late like that. I can't think about that now,' said Frankie, her voice choked with emotion.

'OK. Don't get upset. Where's Sharon now?'

'Still inside. She's in bits. The kids are at home, being looked after by a neighbour. I'll have to go back soon, but I thought I should let you know.'

'When did it happen?' asked Margaret, now fully awake and searching her bedside table for her cigarettes and lighter.

'About midnight. A bloke in a truck he'd just over-taken saw it all. He called the police and ambulance.'

'And you just phoned me now? You took your time.'

'Christ Mags. What's the matter with you? They had to get in touch with Sharon, then she called me. We had to sort out the kids and get here, identify the body, all that old bollocks. This is the first chance I've had.'

'Sorry. What about Roxie?'

'I haven't told anyone else. I'll get in touch with her tomorrow.'

Margaret lit a Silk Cut and breathed out smoke. 'You're not going to wake *her* up then.'

'She's in bloody Spain, you're in London. She's prob-ably out on the razz, knowing her and what can she do tonight anyway? Next thing you'll be asking why Sharon didn't call you first.'

'OK, OK.'

'It's always about you isn't it? You bitch when I call you, and you'd have bitched more if I hadn't. Same old Mags.'

'Yeah, yeah, yeah,' said Margaret. 'I'm sorry, I don't mean to snap at you. I am really shocked at what's happened to Monty. It's just that I haven't been sleeping.'

'You never did. Not even as a baby, mum said.'

Mags didn't want to think about the memories her

sister's words dredged up. 'Do you want me to come down?'

'If you want.' Frankie's voice was flat.

'Don't be so enthusiastic will you. She is *my* sister too.'

'And when did you last see her? Or the kids?' said Frankie, pointedly.

'I dunno. Christmas I suppose. Let's not start all that.' Mags felt the familiar animosity rising towards her sister and worked at keeping it in check. 'I'll get dressed, and come down. I'll go to… Where you going to be?'

'At Sharon's. Do you remember the address?'

'Cut it out, will you. Now's not the time. I'll be down in a few hours.'

'You all right to drive?' said Frances, her tone softening.

'I'll manage.'

'Well, take it easy, sis. We don't want another accident tonight, do we?'

'I'll be okay. I'll see you soon,' and with that Margaret put down the phone, her heart full of sympathy for Sharon and her two fatherless children.

2

Frankie winced as the phone banged down at the other end. Bitch, she thought. But our bitch, and she was used to it. As the eldest of the four sisters, she'd taken over as mother when Queenie had succumbed to the breast cancer she'd hidden for so long. Roxie, the youngest of her daughters, was just six years old. Frankie had married, but the experience was short lived, and after the divorce she'd moved to Guildford to be close to Sharon, her husband Monty and their two young children – Peter and Susan, the same two kids who were now in the care of a neighbour. Jesus, would the Doyles ever be happy? she thought as she dropped her cigarette end and crushed it under her foot before straightening her shoulders and heading towards the main doors of the hospital, the sound of the siren from an incoming emergency blatting off the walls. The sound reminded her of one of her many fallings out with her sister. Two years after Queenie's death, Mags, then just thirteen years old, had done a runner one Saturday afternoon.

She was in big trouble at school, but that was nothing new. Mags was precociously attractive, and one day she'd got dolled up in short skirt, black tights, high heels and a low-cut top and headed for the West End. Though she looked five years older than her age in the get-up, she was still an innocent, in a place that fed on innocence. Mickey was useless, but that was becoming a regular thing, and Frankie had to take charge. She headed for Soho and scoured the streets, searching the seedy backstreet dives for her young sister, but when she still hadn't found her after a day of looking, Frankie went to the nearest police station and explained her predicament. For once, the name Doyle didn't ring any bells. But south London was a long way away, and her obvious distress got her a ride in a police car with a constable driving, and a WPC in the back seat with Frankie next to her, through the narrow, busy streets between Oxford Street and Shaftesbury Avenue. Then she spotted Mags outside a record shop that specialised in urban music. She was smoking, and chatting to two boys, one black, one white, both in their late teens and dressed in baggy jeans, hoods pulled down over their eyes and swamped in oversized basketball shirts. 'Thirteen, you say?' said the driver of the car. 'Looks a lot older,' he said, looking at her long legs in her short skirt. He hit a switch on the dashboard and the lights and siren came on, the sound deafening between the buildings. Frankie jumped out of the car and screamed at Mags – the two boys took one look at the situation and melted away down a narrow alley. Frankie snatched the cigarette from between Mags' fingers and threw it into the gutter, then dragged her sister into the police car where she sat stone-faced in the back seat between her and the female officer. Once back at the station, Frankie pushed Mags into a cab, and they headed home in silence. Bitch, thought Frankie, as she had so many times before.

Dragging her mind back to the present day, and the tragic situation that was unfolding, Frankie entered the hospital building again. Sharon was sitting alone in an orange plastic chair in the main reception and Frankie's heart went out to her. Her sister, four years her junior, was leaning forward, white faced, elbows on knees with a crumpled tissue held tightly in her hand. Frankie sank into the hard plastic seat next to her, as the business of the hospital – frantic even at that late hour – went on around them. Frankie put one hand on Sharon's clenched fist. 'We should get back to the house love,' she said. 'There's a lot to do, and Mags is coming down from London.'

Sharon shook her head. 'Why?' she asked in a voice made husky from grief. 'Why Monty?'

'Don't ask me duck,' said Frankie, using Queenie's pet name for all the girls. 'I don't know.'

'He looked so peaceful, just like he was asleep,' said Sharon, the words disappearing into a sob.

'I know.'

'What am I going to tell Peter and Susan?'

'The truth. That's all you can do. I know it's going to be hard for you. I'll help.' Frankie thought of the children she had doted on since they were tiny babies.

'But they're so young, and now no dad.' Peter was nine, Susan seven.

'It was like that for us when mum went,' Frankie said. 'Worse, what with Roxie being so young, and poor dad left alone with the four of us.'

'He had you.'

'I was thirteen, remember.'

'Thirteen going on thirty-three. You looked after all of us, dad included.'

And lost my teenage years, thought Frankie, and my chance of a university education – although she held no bitterness towards her family. At least, not much. After her mother's death she'd adapted to caring for her sisters and her father, who had lapsed into a sadness that he'd never recovered from. Frankie had quickly become head of the household. She'd persevered at school, taken some exams, but moving away was out of the question. Her A-levels were good enough, but instead of a carefree time with her peers, she'd applied to a local bank and ended up behind a counter, a name tag pinned to her chest.

Their father had gone into a decline, and died of heart failure – or more likely a broken heart – when Frankie was nineteen and Roxie was twelve. The firm had splintered without Queenie's leadership, and Frankie became a wage slave just to keep the house going. Her youngest sister had lived with her for a few years, before Frankie's marriage. Roxie trained as a beautician in central London and worked in a few salons servicing pampered yummy mummies, before getting a job on a luxury cruise ship until finally, she bought a small beauty salon in Spain. Frankie had never forgiven herself for taking the easy way out and marrying the first bloke who'd asked her. It had been an unhappy marriage from day one, and her husband, John Foster had made it clear that he came first, not the family. After a period when Frankie had been out of touch with her sisters, she dumped her job and her husband, and ended up back in the bosom of her family.

'And I'll look after you now. You've got me and Mags here,' said Frankie, trying to reassure her.

'Mags will be a fat lot of good, knowing her.'

'You might be surprised when push comes to shove.'

'After what's happened?'

'Let's not talk about that now. Let's get you home and get some rest.'

'*Rest*,' Sharon almost shouted. 'How can I rest with Monty here?'

'You have to. There's arrangements to be made,' said Frankie. 'I'm sorry but there are. I'll help, and so will Mags I know.'

'They're going to cut him up,' sobbed Sharon.

'Try not to think about it,' said Frankie.

'I can't help it,' said Sharon. 'I know it's the law. It's just not fair,' wailed Sharon.

'Come on sis. There's nothing more we can do here 'til the morning.'

'That policeman said…'

'He said he'd come round and see you. I'll be there, and Mags will know what to do.'

'I suppose so,' said Sharon, slowly. As she got up she stumbled, and her sister righted her. Still holding Sharon, Frankie led them slowly out of the building, towards the car park.

It seemed to Frankie that she had spent most of her life supporting one or more members of her family since Queenie's death. Driving back to Sharon's house, her sister sobbing in the passenger seat, Frankie felt the years drop away one by one as the street lights phased across the bonnet of the car. First it was Mickey. The good father the girls had always known, quick with a joke, generous with money and slow to anger, changed that dreadful first winter. First it was the booze. He started drinking when he got up at noon, and stayed pissed until he fell into bed in the early hours after playing Queenie's favourite records on the stereo in the basement. Even then, sometimes he didn't make it as far as his bed, and Frankie would find him curled up on the stairs when she got up at six in order to get the other girls ready for school. She'd wake him and help him to his room, but often he'd turn on her, and sometimes even became violent, a secret she managed to keep from her sisters for years. Other times she'd discover him in a pool of vomit, which she quietly cleaned up, then simply covered him with a blanket and went back to her other chores.

Then there were the girls themselves. Sharon was easy. No trouble. Although Frankie knew she missed her mother dreadfully. But Mags and Roxie were a handful. The Soho incident being just one of Mags' misde-meanours. Then Roxie began to grow up, and she followed Mags' example. Mags would stay out all night clubbing, and Roxie did exactly the same as she matured into a teenager. Which left Frankie as the stay at home skivvie. Mickey's behaviour had got worse and he used to vanish for days on end. Often Frankie would find strange women in the house and in fact it was a blessing when her father passed away. One less to manage, she secretly thought, although she was ashamed at her disloyalty.

3

After she'd put down the phone Margaret Doyle leant back on the headboard of her bed in her Battersea flat. Christ, she thought. What a turn up for the books. Monty; dead. She couldn't deny that he'd been a pain in the arse sometimes, pompous and pedantic, but then, that was a by-product of his job and she knew that he'd loved Sharon and their children. Bought them a big house, and they were never short. But then he was an accountant, and she'd never come across a poor one yet. She took another swig of water and saw that her hand was shaking. Just what I need, she thought, a drive to Guildford at this time of night. She shook her head, berating herself. Frankie was right, she thought. Still the same old selfish Mags. She swung herself out of bed, and headed for the shower, dressed just in yesterday's knickers. On the way she opened her bedside drawer and extracted a wrap of white powder. Something for the road, she thought, as she cut out a fat line with a credit card and snorted it up one nostril. Thank God there'd been no search of the flat when she'd been suspended from her job as a Detective-Sergeant with the Met. They wouldn't have liked what they would've found.

Once showered, the coke already making her feel more alert, she wiped the bathroom mirror clear of steam and took a long look at herself. She still had the Celtic colouring of thick black hair that made her blue eyes stand out. Still the heart-shaped face with just a few laughter lines. Not bad for nearly thirty she thought, and winked at her reflection. After all I've been through too. She left the bathroom and dressed in clean underwear, jeans and a hooded sweatshirt, and wondered whether to pack some clothes. Would it be a long visit? Better safe than sorry, so she jammed underwear, a skirt and another sweater into a small bag, hid the remains of the cocaine in a side pocket and pulled on a pair of ankle boots. Grabbing her car keys, she headed for the door, wide eyed. On the way out she looked at the gun cabinet bolted to a support wall. Her service weapon had never been returned to her after she'd been suspended, but inside the cabinet – under a false bottom that a good friend had built into the box – were her personal, and highly illegal weapons. A Colt .45 semi automatic pistol and a Colt Commander .38 revolver, plus ammunition for both. No, she thought, shaking her head. I don't need to be armed where I'm going.

She went outside and found her Porsche Boxter, her one extravagance, parked where she'd left it, got inside and headed south, back to Guildford.

4

A false dawn was touching the top of the hills above Guildford when Sharon and Frankie finally returned from the hospital. Frankie turned the car into the short drive that led up to Sharon's detached house. All the downstairs lights were on. She parked up and they walked together to the front door which was slightly ajar. Inside the house, Marion, Sharon's next door neighbour – was on the phone in the hallway, talking quietly. 'They're here,' she said into the mouthpiece, and offered the phone to Sharon. 'It's your sister Margaret,' she said. 'She's on her way.'

Sharon shook her head and instead walked into the lounge where she fell heavily into an armchair. Frankie took the receiver. 'Mags, we're home now. How long will you be?'

She listened. 'See you then,' and put down the phone gently. She smiled at Marion and said. Thanks love, don't know what we'd have done without you.'

'Do you want me to stay?' Marion asked.

'No, you've done enough. Go get some sleep.'

'If I can. This is horrible. How is Sharon holding up?'

'I'm not sure it's hit her properly yet.'

'Poor love. I'll just go and say goodbye to her.'

Marion went into the lounge and said, biting her lip. 'Sharon, the kids are asleep. I just looked in. I'm so sorry, I don't know what to say.'

'Thanks,' said Sharon, staring out into space, the fatigue and grief showing deeply on her face. She had aged ten years in the last few hours.

'Listen, do you need them taken to school or anything? I can drop them off.'

Sharon looked at Frankie who was standing in the doorway, her expression blank. It was left to Frankie to answer Marion. 'I don't know if they'll go tomorrow.'

'Well, just let me know. You've got all my numbers.'

Sharon nodded and Frankie herded her towards the front door. 'Thanks again, we'll be in touch.'

'Anything,' replied Marion. 'I mean it. We're just next door, and Monty is – was – such a good man.'

Frankie nodded as she closed the front door behind her. She leant up against it, and despite herself, started to cry for the first time that night.

She shook her head at her own weakness, dried her eyes with a hanky from her coat pocket, and went back into the lounge where Sharon had fallen asleep in a chair. Frankie took off her coat and tucked it round her sister. That's the right thing to do, she thought, sleep while you can. Frankie then went upstairs to check on her nephew and niece who were sleeping peacefully in their beds. Not much peace for you for a while thought Frankie, as she gently closed the doors to their rooms.

She went back into the kitchen, where she put on the kettle for a pot of tea. On the way downstairs she passed the family photographs lined up on the walls. The family all pictured together in happy times, holidays at the villa in Spain, Christmas here and at Sharon's previous, smaller house. She could hardly bear to look at them. There were even a couple with her in attendance, although she could not remember on what occasion. So much for me, she thought.

She sat at the kitchen table sipping the hot brew as the sky outside lightened, until she heard the sound of a car pulling up outside. She went to the front door as Margaret parked next to her car and got out. 'Hello Mags,' said Frankie as the sisters embraced.

'Hello yourself,' said Margaret. 'This is not good.' She spoke in a low voice so as not to disturb the quiet of the empty street.

'You can say that again,' came Frankie's reply, equally hushed.

'Where's Sharon?'

'In the lounge, asleep in a chair. She's exhausted.'

'Christ. Poor bloody Monty.'

'*You* never thought much of him.'

'I don't think much of anybody,' said Margaret. 'Except you lot of course.'

'That's why we never see you?' said Frankie, her tone accusatory.

'Don't start Frankie. Not today. You know that's not true. Anyway, even if it is, I'm here now aren't I?'

'I'm sorry darling. This is all beginning to get to me.'

'And we haven't even begun yet,' said Mags in a gloomy voice.

'How do you mean?'

'If he was pissed. You know how it goes. Postmortem. The whole nine yards.'

'Oh God don't say that!' said Frankie, thinking of Monty's cold body laid out on a mortuary slab.

'Come on,' said Roxie, trying to lighten the mood. 'I want to get inside and drop my bags off. And I'm dying for a cuppa.'

'Well you're in luck, I just made some. And I've got some breakfast on the go too.'

'Trust you. No I'm not hungry,' said Mags, thinking of the coke in her bag.

They went inside, peeped in at Sharon who was still asleep and snoring gently, then went into the kitchen where Frankie poured them both a cup of tea. 'A teapot,' said Margaret. 'Don't see many of those these days. It's usually a tea bag in a mug for me.'

'Domestic,' said Frankie, sarcastically.

'Yeah,' replied Margaret. 'Just like home.'

'This is a home.'

'Not any more. Not for a while,' said Margaret sadly. 'You remember.'

Sharon nodded, both of them thinking back to the dreadful day they buried their mum.

The lead hearse had carried Queenie Doyle's coffin with one display of white roses reading QUEENIE, one reading MUM lying on each side of it. Mickey and the four girls were in the car behind. He wore a long, black coat over a black suit, with a white shirt tightly buttoned at the neck, and a black tie. His four daughters were decked out in black berets, new black coats, black tights, and shiny black shoes, all chosen by Queenie's sister.

Behind them was a long queue of expensive cars, such a convoy that it jammed the traffic in the Norwood Road whilst the girls and Mickey sat weeping. Little Roxy hadn't even understood what was happening but had cried hot tears at the sight of her sisters and daddy so upset. The vicar didn't know the family, but did his best during the short service. Friends and relatives said a few words, hymns were sung, prayers were said, and the congregation left as Judy Garland sang *Over the Rainbow* from the speaker system. The earth was frozen solid that winter, and a mechanical digger had ripped the grave from the dirt. The crowd, featuring almost every south London villain not currently banged up at Her Majesty's pleasure, stood shivering as the vicar intoned his last words, and the family tossed more white roses onto the lid of the coffin as the vicar threw in a handful of soil. As the mourners walked back to the cars, they heard the sound of the digger firing up its engine, ready to fill in the grave. Mickey was inconsolable, and Frankie held his head on her shoulder as his tears soaked her new coat. The other girls huddled together for comfort as the car drove them back home for the wake, where the drinking would carry on until the small wee hours. There was a spread laid out like a royal banquet, laid on by some 'business associates'. Everyone wanted to show their respects to the Queen.

It had been a cheerless Christmas for the family as Queenie succumbed to the cancer that had spread throughout her body. There had been talk of a double mastectomy, but the doctors had discovered that the disease had moved to her liver, kidneys and spleen. They said that if she'd gone to her doctor when she first discovered the lumps, they could have saved her, but it was too late. She discharged herself from hospital and went home. Private nurses cared for her night and day, but there was no hope. The house stank of the flowers delivered by friends and family. None of the girls would ever disassociate the smell from those terrible days. Then, on Christmas Eve, she passed away. Presents were left unopened. The turkey rotted in the fridge. The end of an era.

Now, listening to Sharon's soft weeping, Mags remembered those dark days. 'Here we go again,' said Mags. 'After dad, I thought it would be a long time until another funeral.'

'Never long enough,' said Frankie.

'It's going to be hard for them. For all of us.'

Frankie nodded. 'It's after the funeral that it's really rough.'

And that wasn't the half of it, thought Frankie, remembering the bad times with Mickey and the girls. The bad times she protected them from, no matter how badly Mags and Roxie treated her. No matter how many times she felt Mickey's open handed slaps and some-times his fist, she reminded herself that it was only her standing between him and her sisters. 'You remind me so much of her,' he would sob. 'I don't mean to hurt you. Sometimes I wish it had been you that died.'

Those words had been worse than the punches, and Frankie kept them locked away in a part of her mind she didn't often visit.

'We'll get them through it,' was all she said. 'I'm going for a smoke.' She wanted to be alone for a while.

5

Outside in the back garden, Frankie lit up a cigarette and took a long drag, pulling a face at the taste, and Mags' words. Of course she remembered. How could she ever forget those last months of her mother's life, and what followed? The cancer that had gripped the woman she loved most in the world. The weeks on the wards where she learned to hate the stink of them, so the memories came flooding back last night as she and Sharon entered Guildford hospital. The bad food left uneaten as Queenie's chemo shrank her appetite to nothing. Helping her mother to the toilet where the blood covered stools made her want to vomit. Her father, just sitting holding his wife's hand stone-faced, unable to articulate his feelings. The other three girls, not believing what was happening, and in Roxie's case, hardly knowing. Frankie grew up overnight as she was forced to take on the responsibilities of the household. Cooking, cleaning, washing, ironing, looking after the girls and her father with little or no help, although Mags tried her hardest, and even little Roxie, helped out – or tried to. Frankie still remembered how her attempt to make breakfast one Sunday almost burned the house down when the toast caught fire.

No, Frankie would never forget how a home had changed into a prison where she strived to do her school work as well as look after everyone. Social workers hovered, determined to split up the family but her dad had succeeded in keeping them together with help from the Doyles' extended family – coming close to violence several times – until the social left them alone, and Frankie became queen of the house. But not the real queen. She could never be replaced.

'Course I remember,' she said to herself. 'Hard not to.'

6

Dawn had well and truly broken and the sisters were back sitting at the kitchen table when they heard a sound outside the door and a sleepy headed Peter stuck his head round the door. 'Why is mummy asleep in the lounge?' he asked, then, 'Aunty Mags, is that you?' he said, his smile beaming wide with delight.

Margaret got to her feet and went to the boy. 'Hello Peter,' she said.

'Hello. I didn't know you were coming.' he said excitedly. 'Where's dad? He's not in bed.'

Margaret hugged the boy, and looked round at her sister for guidance. 'Frankie,' she said, not knowing what to say to the boy.

Frankie got up from her seat. 'Peter,' she said softly. 'Come here, lovey.'

He went to his other aunt, looking even more bewildered.

Frankie led him to a chair at the kitchen table and sat him down. 'Dad's gone away for a bit,' she said, wishing

Sharon was there. 'We've all had a late night and mum's very tired.'

'Gone where?' the boy asked. 'Where did you go last night? We were scared.'

'We'll explain later. Now be a good big boy, and don't ask questions. Do you want some breakfast?'

Peter nodded, but he was smart and sensed that something was wrong. 'Shall I go and wake Susan?' he asked his aunts.

'Leave her for now,' said Frankie.

'What about school?' he insisted. 'It's my turn to feed the guinea pig today.'

'You're having a day off. A holiday,' said Margaret. 'I'll go and wake your mum.'

She left the room, glad to be away from her nephew and his questions. Ever since he'd been able to understand what she did for a living, he'd hero-worshipped her. He loved watching crime series on TV, although Sharon put her foot down on letting him look at the ones containing sex and violence. But even so he managed to watch as many as he was allowed, and was sure that Aunty Mags was a mixture of Wonder Woman, Cagney and Lacey and Miss Marple, all rolled into one. Mags wished she could have lived up to his ideas about her, but she knew this was just the beginning. She reached the lounge where Sharon was still asleep and Margaret hated to wake her to the worst day of her life, but the children would need her. She shook her sister and Sharon jumped, suddenly wide awake. 'Mags,' she said, the memory of what happened last night suddenly hitting her like a ton of bricks. 'It's you. So it wasn't a dream.'

'I'm so sorry sweetie,' said Margaret. 'But it's morning and Peter's up asking questions. And no, it wasn't a dream. I wish it was, for your sake.'

Sharon shoved Frankie's coat off and got up. 'I must look a fright,' she said.

'You were always the best looking one of all of us,' replied Margaret. 'You look fine.'

Sharon glanced in the mirror over the fireplace. 'Right,' she said. 'Look how red and puffy my eyes are. I look like a bloody witch. I'll scare the kids.'

'I doubt it. What will you tell them?'

'The truth, Frankie said I should tell the truth.'

'I didn't know what to say, I told Peter Monty was away.'

'Thanks sis. I understand. You had to tell him something.'

'And I told him that there was no school today.'

'No, that's the right thing to do. I won't send them to school today. Listen, where is he?'

'In the kitchen with Frankie. She's making his breakfast.'

'And Susan?'

'Still asleep.'

'Okay,' said Sharon, looking suddenly more resilient. 'Let me go wash my face and I'll talk to them.'

'I'll be with you. Don't worry,' said Margaret.

'You've done it haven't you? In your job I mean.'

'Breaking bad news is the worst part. But it's got to be done sis, and we'll all be here with you.'

Sharon went upstairs to her bathroom where she quickly splashed cold water on her face in a vain attempt to get the redness out of her eyes. She looked in the mirror as her younger sister had done hours before. 'The best looking one,' she said aloud. 'Oh Monty, why?'

She smoothed down the sweater she was wearing over the blue jeans that she had dragged on when the police had arrived last night. They'd tracked the address from the number plate of Monty's car. 'Well, here goes,' she said under her breath, steeling herself to deliver the news to her children. 'How am I going to cope with this?' And with that, she started to cry.

7

'Stop it,' she said quietly, trying to get herself in check. 'I've got to be strong.' She dried her eyes on a piece of toilet roll and left the bathroom. She went to Susan's room and looked at her youngest child, still asleep, with the covers almost off the bed where she'd kicked them off in the night. She could hardly bring herself to wake Susan, but she knew she had to. 'Sweetheart,' she said, and brushing the hair off her face.

Susan's eyes opened and she smiled. 'Mummy,' she said. 'I had a bad dream.'

'I know, sweetie. So did I.'

'Is it better now?' said Susan, hopefully.

Sharon shook her head. 'Come on love, get up and clean your teeth. Mummy has something to tell you.'

'What? Are we getting a puppy?'

'Oh God,' said Sharon, the lump in her throat threatening to choke her. 'Now come on, Peter's downstairs, and Aunty Frankie and Aunty Mags. they've come to see you.'

'Aunty Mags!' said the child delightedly. 'I haven't seen her for ages.'

'Well she's here now. Put on your dressing gown and we'll go and see her.'

Susan almost leapt out of bed, tugged on her dressing gown and ran to the second bathroom where she scrubbed her teeth, showed them gleaming to her mother and ran downstairs. 'Aunty Mags,' she shouted on the way. 'Where are you?'

Sharon followed slowly, knowing that what she had to say would destroy the child's delight. She shook her head as she went. Please God, she said to herself. Help me.

When she got to the kitchen, Peter was eating corn flakes at the table and Susan was sitting on Margaret's lap, a beaming smile on her face.

Here goes, thought Sharon.

'Peter; Susan,' she said, 'I've got some very bad news.'

The two children looked at her, each with a confused expression on their faces.

'There was an accident last night. Daddy was hurt.'

'No,' said Peter, but Susan just looked even more confused.

'Yes,' said Sharon. 'Now come here darlings, both of you.'

She crouched down to her children and gathered them in her arms. 'Daddy's not coming back my darlings. He's gone to live with the angels now.'

Peter started to cry, and Susan joined in, although she really wasn't quite sure why. At her young age death was something that she didn't understand. It had been the same with Roxie when Queenie died. It had all been too much to take in.

Sharon hugged them to her breast and started to cry too, whilst her two sisters just looked on, faces torn with pity, knowing there was nothing they could do to stop the pain.

8

———◆———

Frankie was the first to disturb her loved ones huddled, weeping on the floor. She jumped up from her chair and rushed over to them. 'Sharon,' she said. 'Why don't you take them upstairs? Take them to your room.'

Sharon looked up at her, tears pouring from her eyes. 'Yes,' she said. 'That'll be good. Upstairs. Somewhere quiet.'

'Quiet is good,' replied Frankie. 'We'll be here. I'll have to phone work. Take some time off.'

Sharon looked at Margaret. 'And you?' she asked.

'As long as you need me, love,' said Margaret. 'I'm here for you – and you know I don't have anywhere to be at the moment.'

'Thank you, both of you. Come on kids, let's watch TV in Mummy's room.'

The trio left the kitchen, with Margaret and Frankie following them into the hallway, but as Sharon and the children started up the first flight of stairs there was a ring at the doorbell. Through the frosted glass Margaret saw the familiar silhouettes of two uniform caps. One male, one female. 'It looks like the police,' she said. 'I'll deal with this.'

'Will you,' said Sharon. 'I can't face it. If you need me...'

'I'll call you,' said Margaret, and as the three went upstairs she walked to the front door and opened it. Outside was a uniformed police sergeant holding a ziplock bag, and a young WPC. 'Mrs Smith?' he asked.

'Sister. Detective-Sergeant Margaret Doyle of the Met.' She didn't show her ID, because it was still in the flat in Battersea.

'Oh. Good to meet you. Sorry. You know what I mean. I'm Sergeant Turner from Guildford police station. This is WPC Dodds.'

'Hello Sergeant Turner. Hello WPC Dodds. Come in.'

'Can we speak to Mrs Smith?' Turner asked as he came inside the house.

'She's upstairs. She's just told her children what happened and they're in bits, as you can imagine, so I said I'd talk to you.'

'Christ.'

'Yeah, it's been a tough one. Come into the living room.'

The sergeant and the WPC followed Margaret into the room. 'Sit down,' she said. 'Tea? My sister's making some.'

'I thought you said she was upstairs?'

'No Frankie. Our eldest. There's a lot of us.'

'That's good at this sort of time,' said the policeman, obviously uncomfortable in this house of grief. The young woman said nothing, just took out a police-issue notebook.

'It helps to have family around you. Did you want tea, either of you?'

'No, I'll pass,' said the sergeant. The WPC, who looked young, out of her depth, just shook her head. 'I'm glad I'm speaking to you to be honest,' he went on. 'I've never got used to all this, and I've been in the job for twelve years.'

'Me neither,' agreed Mags, thinking of all the times she had been in his shoes.

The pair sat on the sofa, and the sergeant said, 'we pulled the car away from the crash site at first light, and it's being examined at our garage. It's a miracle it didn't catch fire. We found Mr Smith's jacket in the back.' He indicated the bag he'd been carrying. 'It must have fallen off the back seat in the accident. There was a wallet in the inside pocket with cash and cards, and his phone, and what looks like house and office keys. We'll need you to sign for them.'

'Of course.'

'The car keys were still in the ignition of course. It looks like a write-off I'm afraid.'

'That hardly matters now. Sharon has a car of her own but she wouldn't get in that car anyway now.'

The sergeant nodded. 'After that it's just procedure – as you'll be aware,' he said. 'Post mortem We'll be checking for alcohol and drugs in his system as a matter of course. How old are the children?'

'Seven and five.'

'God, that's a tragedy,' he said, thoughtfully.

'You can say that again.'

'Well thank you for your time,' said the sergeant. 'We'll be on our way. Sign here please.' He passed Margaret an official form listing what had been found, and a pen. She dashed off a signature, then he fished a card from his breast pocket. 'If you need me for anything, just call. Normally we'd stick around but you're a copper too. We'll leave you alone for now. But we may have to come back. You know how it is.'

'I do.'

'Sergeant Doyle, thank you.'

'I won't say it was a pleasure.'

'I'm sure.' And with that he got up, put his cap back on and allowed Margaret to see him and the WPC out. She had not spoken in the ten minutes she'd been in the house, but Margaret still felt sorry for her. It won't ever get any better, she thought.

9

In a tiny flat with broken air conditioning on the Costa del Sol, Roxie Doyle sat in the side of her bed dressed in just a pair of knickers, worrying about her lack of customers and money. Suddenly she heard noises from her beauty salon below the flat. 'Christ, what now?' she said aloud as she pulled on a dress and went downstairs.

The salon was situated in a tacky shopping mall, deserted at that early hour, and the front door stood wide open. The shop was empty, aside from the unwelcome sight of her ex-boyfriend Tony Darrow, elegant, but wasted – his grubby cream suit and pink shirt contrasting deeply with the open shiny blade of the flick knife he was holding.

'Tony,' she said. 'What the hell are you doing here?'

'Come for my money love,' he said, in the cockney accent she'd once found so attractive, but now got on her nerves. 'You've been ducking my calls.'

When they were together Tony had loaned Roxie a lot of cash, supposedly for the business, but in fact most had gone on the high life for them both.

'I don't have your money,' said Roxie. 'You spent most of it yourself if you remember.'

'Not my fault you couldn't resist me. But it was a loan, and now I've come to collect.'

'Like I said Tony. I don't have it. Look around. The place is falling apart at the seams. I'm on my own here – most of the time, if you get my drift. Business has fallen off. There's more fashionable places to go. The whole mall is going down the pan. Ex-pats having their houses knocked down, getting old and dying. I've even had to sell my jeep just to pay the rent.'

'Save me the sob story,' said Tony. 'Business is just as bad for me. That's why I need my money back.'

'And if I don't give it to you?'

He held up the knife. 'Then I'm going to fuck you in every hole and then slice that pretty face of yours until your best friend won't recognise you.'

'Run out of best friends Tony. And as for the fucking bit, I hope you're better at it than you used to be. 'Specially in the condition you're in. Couldn't get it up most of the time.'

'What did you say, you cunt?' said Tony, almost dancing in his two-tone shoes with anger and excitement.

'You been at the marching powder again, Tony?' said Roxie.

'I mean it you bitch. Get me my fucking money or I'll cut you up good.' he said.

'Actually I believe you. Listen,' she said, going behind the counter where the shop's till hummed. 'There's some cash in here. It's all I've got.' She pressed a key and the till opened. At the back was a thin bundle of high denomination Euro notes Roxie had been saving for a rainy day. It looked like that day had come. She pulled out the cash and underneath was a nickel plated, pearl handled, single shot .22 Derringer nestling in the plastic tray, fully loaded. A lady's gun – actually a gift from Tony when they were still together. The stuff they were into, Roxie needed it for protection. Luckily Tony obviously didn't remember that she still had it. A purse pistol, but still deadly in the right hands and that morning Roxie's *were* the right hands.

Seeing the few notes, Tony yelled in anger and frustration. 'Peanuts.'

Roxie picked up the pistol, cocked the hammer and shot him in the right eye, the sound of the shot from the tiny gun no louder than a cough. His knife hit the floor before him, but not by much.

Roxie went round his dead body without touching it, and closed the front door.

She stood for a moment looking down at him, a red hole where one eye had been, the other blown out on its stalk by the concussion from the bullet, when the phone on the counter rang. It was Frankie with the bad news about Monty.

It must be Fate, she thought, as she put the phone down. I definitely need to leave the country – and quickly. She put the phone down, went upstairs, dressed, packed, took the money she'd saved, stepped over Tony's body, went out to the mall, locked up the shop behind her and went looking for a cab. On the way, she carefully wiped her fingerprints off the gun and dropped it down an open drain.

10

Margaret went back into the kitchen where Frankie was again sitting at the table, looking half dead, yet another cup of sweet tea in front of her. 'Do those coppers want a drink?' she asked.

'No, they've gone.'

'What's that you've got?' asked Frankie.

'They brought these,' said Mags, laying Monty's wallet, top of the range BlackBerry and keys on the table, and hanging the jacket on the back of a chair. 'Monty's stuff. They found them when they recovered the car.'

'Christ, how could he be so stupid,' said Frankie. 'How could he?'

'Accidents happen.' God knows she'd seen enough in her job.

'But he did drink and drive. I know that. All those late night meetings. I begged him not to, for Peter and Susan's sake. I always dreaded something happening to him, and now…' Frankie's voice tailed away.

'He wasn't…?' said Margaret.

'What?'

'Playing away.'

'Course he wasn't!' Frankie exclaimed, angrily. 'Typical copper. Always suspicious.'

'Don't be so naïve. It happens. They'd been married eight years.'

'No way. He loved Sharon and those kids, look at everything he provided for them.'

'I know. That was unfair. It was just a thought.'

'Well keep it to yourself in future, you'll upset Sharon.'

Margaret nodded, then said. 'I'm sorry about this morning on the phone. Jumping down your throat. I've not been sleeping well lately,' she said, looking faintly vulnerable.

'I'm not surprised. Losing your job.'

'I haven't lost it Frankie. At least not yet. I'm suspended.'

'What happened Mags? I know we don't see each other much but you're my little sister and I'm always here for you.'

'I was suspended for shooting the wrong bloke. But he was a waste of space anyway. Wrong time, wrong place. At least he's not dead – though it would be no loss if he was.' Mags looked grim for a moment, then continued. 'But forget that for now. What do we do next?'

Frankie looked at the kitchen clock. 'Half eight,' she said. 'We have to call Roxie. What time is it in Spain? Is it an hour forwards or backwards or the same.'

'Christ, I can't remember. Let's just call her,' Mags said.

'Get rid of that jacket first, in case Sharon comes down. She doesn't need to see it right now.'

'Of course.'

'You'll be in the spare room,' said Frankie. 'The bed's made up.'

'I'll take it upstairs with my bag. We'll tell Sharon later about Monty's things.'

'Take the other stuff too. I've got his watch and ring. They gave them to me at the hospital. Poor Sharon couldn't look.'

'You can't blame her,' said Margaret, as she gathered up Monty's stuff, then went to her car and got her bag, then went upstairs to her room. When she had put his jacket in the wardrobe, unpacked her few things and stashed the cocaine in her shoe, she put Monty's wallet and phone in the drawer of the bedside cabinet, keeping the keys so that she could get in and out of the house, and went back downstairs. On the way she peered into the master bedroom where Sharon, Peter and Susan were lying fast asleep again, on top of the bed, the curtains drawn against the sun.

She rejoined Frankie who looked even more shattered. 'They're all asleep,' she said. 'And so should you be. You look knackered.'

'Things to do first. Let's call Roxie, I've got her number. By the way I just called Joyce.' Joyce was Monty's secretary. A single woman fast approaching retirement age, she had become part of the fabric of the family. 'She couldn't speak she was so upset. Is this how it's going to be?' said Frankie, her eyes misty.

Margaret nodded. 'You know it will, at least for a bit. What about Monty's mother?' she asked.

'I haven't had the heart. You know she's ill?'

Margaret nodded again. 'Do you think she'll be well enough to come down?'

'I don't know. She's all alone up there in Norwich. It'll be a terrible shock. Monty was her only child. I don't know what she'll do.' She looked confused at the phone in her hand. 'What was I doing?'

'Calling Roxie,' said Margaret. 'Or do you want me to?'

Frankie shook her head and, using the phone on the kitchen wall, she dialled the number she took from the diary she kept in her handbag. She listened for a few seconds, then said. 'Roxie, it's Frankie. I know it's early. Listen, listen. This isn't a social call. I've got very bad news.'

A pause.

'It's Monty,' she went on. 'He's dead.'

Another pause.

'A car crash. Can you come over?'

A third.

'You can. Great. It'll be good to see you. Margaret's here. She's staying. You can stay at mine. How soon can you make it?'

A further pause.

'Thanks Dolly. Let us know what time and we'll get you picked up. It'll be good to see you. See you later.' Replacing the receiver, she turned to Mags. 'She'll get the first flight she can. She's got a good manageress at the salon who she can leave in charge. She'll go to Gatwick, and phone when she knows what time she's arriving. You'll pick her up won't you?'

Margaret nodded.

'She sounded strange,' said Frankie.

'Nothing new there. She always sounds strange, our Roxie. Anyway, you just broke bad news.'

'No. Not like always. Even with what I told her. Something's wrong.'

'We'll find out when she gets here. Some bloke or other as usual.'

'Suppose so. I'll stay here. You get some sleep if you can. You don't know how late she'll be.'

'What about you Frankie? You look dead on your feet,' said Margaret.

'I'll manage. I'll sleep later.'

'Come on Frankie, you're always looking after everyone else. You need to take care of yourself too.'

'I'm sure,' said Frankie.

'OK, but I don't know if I can sleep.'

'Try. Now go.'

And Margaret did as she was told.

When she had gone, Frankie put her head on her arms where she sat and finally fell asleep through sheer exhaustion.

11

—————>•<—————

Margaret left the kitchen and headed upstairs to the quiet of her room where she lay on the bed, fully clothed apart from her boots, and pulled the duvet over her. She was used to sleeping with her clothes on in her job, and she tried to doze. Speaking about her suspension had brought back the memory, and she tossed and turned, unable to sleep as she went over the details of that fateful day three months ago.

It had been a big operation. One of the biggest she'd ever been involved in. An operation involving the Met, the revenue, and even some shadowy characters from MI5, although they kept their distance. The bad guys were a mixture of Russian Mafia and homegrown East London hard men. A volatile mix indeed, as the Russians thought the Brits were soft, and the East Londoners resented the Russians muscling in on their territory. Nor their methods, which, even by contemporary standards, were rough and ready. Torture, rape, murder. Anything went. But the rewards were sky high. This gang had fingers in so many pies – drugs, illegal immigrants, prostitution, stolen cars, even booze and cigarettes – bringing them down would be a coup of the highest order, and one that was fraught with danger. The final briefing after months of undercover work of the most dangerous kind was at Limehouse police station near Canary Wharf. Margaret was dressed in monkey boots, jeans, a sweater, flak jacket and baseball cap with police insignia on it. Her Browning .9mm pistol with its fifteen-shot magazine nestled in its leather holster on her hip. Sitting next to her was her Detective Inspector at the time. Tony Utter, known to all as Nutter of the yard – although he'd never been stationed there. It was a nickname the older, heavier man enjoyed, as in reality, it was far removed from his calm, capable personality.

'Are you ready for this?' he said to Margaret in his soft, growly voice.

'As I'll ever be,' she replied, though she could feel the butterflies in her stomach as she said it. But he was the man. The man who'd taken time to mentor Margaret from rookie to DS. 'I met your mother once,' he'd told her on their first meeting. 'I was just a lad in a tall hat. She was the queen. It was something and nothing. A parking ticket. She could have told me to piss off, but she was a real lady. Paid up there and then. I'll never forget. Even called me sir, although I know she was just humouring me.'

'No worries. You'll be fine,' he said. 'Just follow my lead.'

'OK boss.'

The take down was at a warehouse in the Docklands, where a delivery was expected around midnight. But it was no ordinary cargo – the back of the articulated lorry was stuffed with illegal immigrants and uncut cocaine and it had sailed through customs at Harwick that evening off a ferry from France. Only thing was, one of the customs men had fitted a GPS transmitter and now a little red light on the receiver showed the truck heading along the North Circular road towards the rendezvous.

Margaret and Utter sat in the lead car, accompanied by two plain vans full of armed police who were to be first into the building, and the convoy set off.

The warehouse was on a trading estate which, at that time of night, was quiet and deserted. This meant that the cops had to split up their vehicles outside so as not to be obvious.

As the vehicles separated on the main road outside the estate, Utter's radio came to life. A pair of plain clothes officers, one male, one female, were strolling up the road arm-in-arm like lovers, and the woman's voice said. 'Two-Two to Utter. Think we've got a spotter on the service road. One IC one male in a green Transit, reg Tango Four One Four Golf Tango Foxtrot.'

'Roger that,' said Utter, then spoke to one of the men in the back, a DC named Flynn. 'Where's the truck?'

'About four minutes away, stopped. Lights I expect.'

'Right Two-Two,' he said into the radio. 'Target expected in four. Wait, then take out the van when the truck arrives.'

'Roger,' came the reply from the plain clothes female.

'That'll do us,' said Utter. 'We'll pile in after the spotter's ours.'

'I hope it's not just someone waiting for his bird,' said Margaret.

'He'll get a hell of a surprise if it is,' said Utter, then informed the other cops of the plan.

A few minutes later, Flynn said, 'here she comes' as a massive lorry lit up like a Christmas tree ground along the street and turned into the estate. The Ford Transit waiting on the service road flashed its lights once and Utter grunted with satisfaction. 'Gotcha,' he said.

As the truck's taillights diminished in their view the two plain clothes, appeared still holding hands, crossed the road in front of the van, separated, the woman shouted something unintelligible and slapped the man's face. They split up, one heading towards the driver's side, the other the passenger's. Then they turned, drew their weapons and ripped open the van doors. The interior light came on, illuminating the face of a very surprised spotter who lifted his hands above his head. 'Done Guv,' the woman's voice said over the radio. 'He thought he was at the pictures watching us ruck. He had a radio, but he didn't have time to use it.'

'We saw,' replied Utter into his transmitter, 'good job.' Then, 'all units, go, go, go.'

* * *

The convoy swiftly regrouped and sped past the captured Transit, down the service road and arrived at the warehouse just as the huge, razor wired gates were closing. The lead van hit the gates with its strengthened front end crashing back open and they caught up with the artic as it drove through the open roller doors of the warehouse itself. The lead vans broadsided and skidded to a halt, their back doors burst open and a dozen members of SO19, each armed with an automatic rifle, rushed past the lorry's trailer into the warehouse screaming. 'Armed police, stay where you are.'

The gang members inside the building ignored the order and made for the back of the building, pulled weapons from about their persons and started to shoot. The SO19 crew took cover and returned fire. 'Christ,' said Utter. 'A fucking war,' and he leapt from the unmarked car, followed by Margaret, the three DCs in the back, and the team of five in the car behind them.

The fire fight was gathering strength when the ten slid up behind the wagon, guns drawn, and ready for action. Margaret quickly forgot her nerves, and her training kicked in as Utter rolled under the back wheels and shimmied up to the rear of the tractor, engine still running, Margaret close behind, exhaust fumes hot and pungent in her lungs. Utter stopped in front of her, bullets coming from all directions. The last thing she heard him say was, 'cluster fuck,' before a stray bullet blew a hole in his head, all the lights in the warehouse went out, leaving the lights from the truck as the only source of illumination.

Suddenly, the place was plunged into darkness as they were cut, apart from the muzzle flashes from the shootout and the lights from the police vehicles in the car park reflecting through the windows.

Margaret felt warm brain matter and blood on her face and clothes and gagged, just managing not to vomit. 'Utter,' she hissed. 'Are you there?' She knew it was pointless speaking to him as he was obviously dead, but she couldn't help herself. She felt for his pulse, but there was nothing. 'Get a medic,' she screamed to the men behind her, not worrying about giving her position away. 'Utter's hit.' Once again she knew it was futile, but she didn't care.

'Christ,' said Flynn, as he scrambled back, pulling his radio from his pocket and calling for medical assistance.

'Bastards,' said Margaret, and she pushed forward under the tractor.

That was when she saw him. The silhouetted figure of a man coming towards her with what looked like a weapon in his right hand. 'Stop,' she called. 'Stop, or I'll shoot.'

The warehouse was full of smoke from the truck's exhaust and the gunfire, and her ears were ringing from the sound of the shots. The man said something and raised what he was holding – and Margaret fired. He went down and lay still.

* * *

An hour later, the gunfight was over and twelve prisoners waited to be transported to various police stations. Three dead bodies, including Utter, were lined up neatly in black body bags on the concrete floor of the warehouse whilst half a dozen casualties from gunshot wounds were on the way to hospital – including the man Margaret had shot. The remains of Utter's squad gathered together, smoking and pacing the car park, when one of the MI5 group joined them. 'You shot a bloke with a mobile phone,' he said to Margaret.

'Looks like it,' she replied, trying to hide the panic that had risen inside her. She couldn't believe what had happened. Utter, her boss dead, and she had made the most amateur of mistakes.

'He was our inside man,' he said.

'Oh Christ,' said Flynn.

'He should've identified himself,' said Margaret.

'Maybe he tried. Anyway, he was unarmed.'

'Looked like a weapon to me.'

'You were wrong. This isn't over yet.'

'Obviously. See the bag next to him. My guv'nor. See this shit all over me.' She was spotted with blood and the contents of Utter's skull.

'Sorry. But that's no excuse. I'll have to put in a report.'

'Do what the hell you like,' said Margaret and went to Utter's car and sat in the back, trying to remove his remains from herself. Once out of sight of the other officers she started to cry. But she wondered who exactly she was crying for.

12

The next morning Detective-Sergeant Margaret Doyle was summoned to New Scotland Yard. She was introduced to her new DI, a recent transfer from south of the river named Trevor Rice. 'Doyle,' he said. 'Name rings a bell.'

'You might have met some of my family,' she replied, coolly.

'Might have nicked one or two, don't you mean,' he replied with a snide grin.

Margaret's heart sank. Just my luck, she thought. He'd obviously heard all about her family's reputation and wanted to tar her with the same brush. She'd worked so hard to get where she was, to rise above her family's reputation and now it was all about to come crumbling down.

Rice asked her no questions about what had happened. There had already been a full debriefing back at Limehouse nick. Not a happy occasion for anyone and especially Mags, who had tried not to think about the fact that her beloved boss was now lying in the morgue and her career was down the pan. Margaret was sure he had already received the report as he simply suspended her with full pay.

'Nothing personal,' he said, a horrible smile on his face. 'The spooks insisted.'

Liar, thought Margaret, but surrendered her warrant card; her gun had been taken at the scene for ballistics.

She left the Yard, drove over the river, found a parking space in Pimlico and went for a coffee. It was a beautiful morning and she sat outside a little cafe and smoked a cigarette.

So this is it, she thought. Bloody suspended for doing my job.

It had never been easy for Margaret joining the police. She'd left home early, just after leaving school at sixteen. Mostly to get away from her constant battles with Frankie, who had taken to ruling the family with a rod of iron, as Mickey took to the bottle. They'd managed to hang on to the house in Streatham, but barely. Money had become tight as the Doyle firm had splintered after Queenie's death. She really had been the top dog, but times had changed. The old fiefdom didn't work on the streets of south London, as younger, more desperate characters took over the criminal businesses she'd managed like some latter day Boudicca.

Margaret had scraped a living working in shops and restaurants for small wages, and living in rented rooms or shared flats. Then, aged twenty-one she'd applied to the Met, was accepted, and sent to Hendon Police College – but it didn't take long for the story to circulate that one of the new female recruits was a member of the

Doyle family. Queenie Doyle was still a legend, even after almost a decade since her death.

Margaret was pretty well ignored by her peers – except for some of the more cocky young constables who tried to get into her pants. She rebuffed every one, and gained the reputation as either frigid or a lesbian. She lived with that and the snide cracks about leopards changing their spots, and graduated second in her class.

The powers that be sent WPC Margaret Doyle straight to Denmark Hill nick in south London. Margaret always viewed it as someone's idea of a joke.

She walked the streets she'd lived as a girl in her brand new uniform, and took a lot more jokes, especially as twice she was involved in arresting members of her own family. That certainly hadn't gone down well and it took a long time to heal those wounds. Even now, they were estranged from the wider family. But as Mags always remembered, they were nowhere to be seen when Queenie's girls were left without a mother. So fuck 'em, she'd do her job and nick them if they needed to be nicked. She persevered, kept her nose clean, lived in a section house, then fell in love with another copper.

He was a Detective-Sergeant, ten years older than her, and married. The old, old story. Mickey was dead and she needed a daddy. She knew from the off it was a mistake, and still walked right into it. It didn't last – word got around, the sergeant's marriage broke down, and she applied for a transfer to north London. 'Bitch' was added to her CV.

She applied for CID, and got the job. Luckily they didn't listen to the rumours and just looked at how good she was at being a copper. She was transferred again to east London where her cold, aloof, exterior, coupled with her good looks, didn't endear her to anyone. The rumour was that she screwed her way into the job. 'Slag' was added to her CV.

The only way that Margaret knew how to survive was to grow a hard shell on her character, and soon she didn't know how else to act. She seldom crossed the river to visit her family and the occasional line developed into a full grown cocaine habit. She took a firearms course, passed with a perfect score, and soon grew to love the feeling of carrying a pistol on her hip. Any fucker takes the piss from now on, she thought, especially after a line or two of the old marching powder, I'll kill the cunt.

She amassed her own small arsenal of illegal weapons after Dunblane, and often drove to some deserted spot for a bit of shooting practice. Too fucking good, she thought with a bitter grin. It would've been better if I'd missed that sod last night.

She finished her coffee, drove home, snarfed up a line and poured a glass of wine.

'Welcome to the rest of my life,' she said, as she toasted herself in the mirror over her dead fireplace.

13

Margaret woke with a start to see Frankie in the doorway of her room. 'What time is it?' she asked, wiping the sleep from her eyes.

'Two,' replied Frankie.

'In the afternoon?'

'That's right. You've been asleep for hours.'

Margaret shuddered as she remembered the uneasy sleep she had fallen into thinking about the fateful events of three months ago.

'What's up? Are you okay? ' said Frankie.

'Nothing, I just didn't sleep well, that's all.'

'I'm glad I woke you then. Roxie called. Her plane gets in at four.'

'I'd better get moving.' Margaret climbed out from under the duvet and headed for the bathroom. 'I'll see you downstairs,' she said. 'How's Sharon?'

'Not good.'

'I won't be long,' said Margaret.

After showering and dressing quickly, Mags recov-

65

ered her stash of coke and took a hit that opened her eyes wide. She wiped her nose and went down to find the rest of the family in the lounge. The TV was turned to CBBC with the sound off, and altogether it was a cheerless sight, with Sharon, Peter and Susan huddled together on the sofa. Outside, it had started to rain.

'I'd better be off soon,' said Margaret. 'Friday afternoons on the motorway are crazily busy, and it's pouring with rain.'

Sharon nodded, and Frankie called out, coming in from the kitchen, 'anything to eat or drink before you go?'

Margaret shook her head. The fact was, she couldn't wait to get away from the house full of sadness. She berated herself inwardly for the thought. 'It'll be good to see Roxie again,' she said as she got her coat.

'How long *has* it been?' asked Sharon, still slumped on her sofa.

'Ages. Birthday and Christmas cards, but that's it for almost two years.'

'We were going to go out to Spain to see her this summer, the whole family...' Sharon started to cry.

'Be strong love,' said Frankie. 'For them,' she said, gesturing towards the kids cuddled up to Sharon, 'if not for all of us.'

'Sorry,' said Sharon, fighting back the tears.

'I'll be going then,' said Margaret, and found her keys in her pocket.

'Drive carefully,' said Sharon. The words hung heavy in the room.

'I will.'

Frankie followed Margaret outside, and they stood in

the shelter of the porch. 'It's been bloody awful,' she said. 'Tears and more tears.'

'Get used to it,' said Margaret. 'There's plenty more where they came from.' The words slipped out before she had a chance to stop them and she cursed herself inwardly.

'At least Roxie might cheer the place up. You know her. It'll be so good for us all to be together again,' Frankie said, forlornly.

Margaret nodded, kissed her sister on the cheek and picked her way through the rain to her car.

14

The drive from Guildford to Gatwick Airport was grim. Margaret couldn't get last night's thoughts out of her head, and the rain, which got progressively worse, didn't help. As usual, the Friday afternoon traffic was monstrously heavy, huge trucks throwing up spray that threatened to drown her windscreen wipers. There was an accident at one point which narrowed the road and brought her speed down to single figures, so that a drive that should have taken an hour took more than two. It was past four o'clock when she finally dumped the Porsche in the short term car park at the airport. Once upon a time, her warrant would have allowed her to park anywhere, but times had changed, she thought ruefully, as she made the long walk to the arrivals lounge for European passengers.

She spotted Roxie right away. Her hair was even more blonde now, cut into a stylish bob her face tanned, and she had a flash looking mobile stuck to her ear. 'Oi,' said Margaret, smiling at her baby sister. 'Long time no see.'

'She's here,' said Roxie into the mouthpiece. 'See you later, bye,' and she cut off the phone and stuck it in the pocket of her immaculately tailored jacket. 'Mags,' she said, brightly, a huge grin on her face. 'Oh Mags. It's so good to see you. No. No. Not like this. You know what I mean.'

'You too Dolly,' said Margaret, using everyone's special name for the baby of the family. 'I haven't seen a smile for a long time.'

'I'd better knock it on the head then,' said Roxie. 'What's it like at Sharon's?'

'About as bad as it can get.'

'I don't know what to say.'

'No one does. So no one speaks much.'

'How are the kids?' Roxie asked, frowning.

'Shellshocked. They remind me of how we were when mum passed.'

'Yeah I remember, even though I was only little at the time. How's Frankie doing? She was always close to Sharon and Monty.'

'Being mum as always. Holding everyone together.'

'Typical. That's what she does best. And what about you? Still going for cop of the year?'

'You know me Dolly. Skating on thin ice as usual.'

'How's work for Her Majesty?'

'Not good. I'm on the shit list. That's why I could get away easily. I've been suspended.'

'What, you – super cop? I don't believe it. What happened?'

'It's a long story. I'll tell you all about it over a glass of Pinot Grigio some time. Anyway, you look well.'

'And doing well,' Roxie lied. 'The salon's going a

bomb. All those old ex-pats wives wanting to look seventeen again. I'm doing Botox, chemical peels, fillers, the lot.'

'I'm glad to hear it. Well come on then, let's go and face the music,' said Margaret.

Roxie wheeled along her suitcase bag, slung her handbag over her shoulder and they made their way back to the car park. 'How long can you stay?' asked Margaret on the way.

'As long as necessary,' replied Roxie. Christ, forever, she thought. Can't go back there in a hurry. In fact never. A dead body on the floor of my shop would be hard to explain. 'Josie, my manageress, is a diamond. She'll look after things for the duration. I haven't had a holiday in years.' She'd let Josie go two months previously, when she could no longer afford to pay wages. More lies, but Roxie was an expert. And being a copper – even a copper on suspension – Margaret probably wouldn't under-stand.

'This won't be much of a holiday I warn you,' her sister reminded her.

'You know me Mags, I could always find some fun and games. And talking of fun and games, how's your love life?'

Margaret pulled a face. 'Don't ask,' she said.

'But I will. Over that glass of wine maybe.'

71

15

The drive back was better than the journey out, as most traffic seemed to be heading in the opposite direction, out of the city for the weekend and the rain had eased off. 'Nice wheels,' Roxie said when she climbed into the Porsche. 'Bet it goes like the clappers.'

'It does. But I don't need any tickets to add to my troubles, so don't go getting any ideas,' said Margaret.

'Can I have a go sometime? I wouldn't mind one of these.'

'Hmmm, we'll see about that. What are you driving?'

'A jeep. Open top. You should come out when this is all over. We'd have some fun.' More lies and Roxie hated doing it – but she knew it was necessary.

'I haven't had any fun for a long time,' Margaret said quietly.

'Poor Mags,' said Roxie. 'I'll make it better.'

They spent the rest of the journey catching up on the last few years, Roxie telling her sister funny stories about some of the clients she had at the salon.

'Sis, you think it's hard catching criminals? Try doing a Brazilian on a 64-year-old woman!'

For her part, Mags traded stories about life on the force. But they both kept more to themselves than they dared to reveal.

They were back at the house just after six, and Frankie, looking worse than ever, opened the front door. She embraced Roxie, and stepped back. 'My, but you look good,' she said, taking in her little sister's highlighted hair, deep tan and inch-long acrylic nails.

'It's more than I can say for you,' said Roxie taking in the deep circles around her eyes. 'You running yourself ragged as usual I suppose?'

'Someone had to look after the family.'

'Well, I'm here now, you can get some rest. Mags said you haven't stopped.'

'I'm OK.'

'Rubbish. When I've seen Sharon and the kids, I'm going to take you home and get you to bed.'

Frankie just nodded, as if she was too tired to argue.

'Where are they?` asked Roxie.

'Sitting down.'

Roxie dropped her bag and went into the lounge where Sharon and her children were still sitting together on the sofa. 'Sharon,' she cried. 'Petey, Soo-Soo.' And she went to them and tried to hold them all.

'Roxie,' said Sharon. 'Thank God you're here.'

Roxie fitted herself on the sofa, her arms around all three, and all four started to cry. 'Sorry,' said Roxie. 'I didn't want to upset you. But...'

Susan snuggled up into her lap and Peter hid his head on her shoulder whilst Sharon hugged her neck.

'It's better now,' said Roxie. 'We'll make it better, all of us together.'

16

As promised, Roxie took Frankie home in her car, and after a supper of takeaway pizza, which the adults picked at and the children wolfed down, Sharon put the children to bed early in her room. She came downstairs to find Margaret sitting in the kitchen with a glass of wine. 'Joyce came round after you left,' she said. 'It was awful. She couldn't stop crying. She saw she was upsetting the children, so she went. I felt terrible letting her go back to an empty house, but what could I do?'

'Nothing,' said Margaret. 'At times like these, everyone has to mourn in their own way. Later, we can mourn together.'

'But she was so much a part of us,' said Sharon. 'You know that. She had nobody else. She's been with Monty so long, she looks on Peter and Susan like her grandchildren.'

'We'll see her tomorrow,' said Margaret. 'We'll sort her out. I promise.'

It was quiet in the house. During the day Frankie had

called up friends and family to tell them the news, and the phone had been busy with outgoing and incoming calls. But Margaret had insisted on switching all the phones off now that the kids had gone to bed, except the one in Monty's study attached to an answering machine. She'd also turned off all the mobiles in the house. 'You need some peace tonight,' she said to Sharon. 'Tomorrow will be a busy day.'

She didn't realise how right she was.

'Want some?' she asked Sharon, tapping the wine bottle as her sister sat down at the kitchen table.

Sharon shook her head.

'Don't mind if I finish the bottle?' asked Margaret. 'It's been a long day.'

'Help yourself,' came the reply. 'Have as much as you like.'

Sharon got up and started to make coffee. 'I don't know what I'm going to do,' she said, in a daze.

'I know it will be hard love but you've got to persevere,' said Margaret, gently. 'You've got Peter and Susan to think about.'

'It's not going to be easy. Monty was my rock. He was the only man I'd ever known.'

'You've got us.'

'For how long? You'll have to go back to London and sort yourself out. And Roxie will fly away back to Spain. She's got a life out there.'

'There's always Frankie.'

'Always Frankie. That's it isn't it. The only one of us without a life of her own.'

'She loves us all. You know that. That's what she does – look after people. '

'I know. Sorry. It's just been another hard day. I'm going to drink this and go upstairs,' said Sharon. 'The kids are in with me tonight. You staying down here?'

'I'll take my glass and watch some crap TV if you don't mind,' said Margaret.

'Whatever you want,' said Sharon as she left the room.

* * *

Next morning dawned bright and breezy, with clouds scudding across a bright blue sky. Under normal circumstances, it was the kind of morning that made you glad to be alive, but the good mood didn't filter through to the house in Guildford. Margaret was the first one up, and after a swift shower and a short line chopped out on the dressing table, she went down to prepare the house for another difficult day.

On the way she looked in on Sharon and the children. Peter and Susan were in bed asleep, but Sharon was standing by the window gazing out. When she heard the door, she turned, her face was drawn and white. 'Hello Mags,' she said. 'Couldn't sleep.'

'Me neither. Just a bit anyway. I'm going to make breakfast. Want some?'

'Just coffee.'

'What about the kids?'

'Orange juice and cereal if they can eat.'

'They have to. They're more resilient than us. You saw them with the food last night. You too. You have to keep your strength up at a time like this.'

'I'll survive.'

'Are you going to wake them?'

'I thought I'd let them sleep for a bit. I could hear Peter crying in his sleep last night.'

'Poor little mites. I'll go and get the kettle on,' said Margaret, gently closing the door behind her.

She laid the kitchen table and when the coffee was steaming Sharon, now dressed, joined her. 'That smells good,' she said, pouring a cup. 'I've left the kids.'

Margaret nodded, and just then they heard the front door open and Frankie, now looking better, and Roxie joined them. Frankie looked better than she had the day before, the dark rings under her eyes having faded slightly.

'Coffee,' said Roxie. 'Bloody great.' She kissed Sharon and Margaret and poured two more cups.

'I'd better switch the phone back on and check for messages,' said Sharon, and as she got up to go to the study the front doorbell rang.

'I'll get it,' said Margaret. 'You check the phone.'

She went to the front door where she found a man in his mid-thirties standing on the porch. 'Detective-Inspector Mahoney,' he said, showing his warrant card. 'Guildford CID. Mrs Smith?'

'No, I'm her sister,' said Margaret. 'Margaret Doyle. Detective-Sergeant.'

'Ah,' he said. 'Detective-Sergeant Doyle. I know about you.' The way he said it, and the insolent way he grinned, made Margaret think he didn't much like what he'd heard. But she didn't care. Straightening her back, she looked him in the eye and said. 'I'm sure you do. What can we do for you?'

'I need to speak to Mrs Smith,' he said.' Something's come up.'

'I'm her sister. You can talk to me.'

'Sorry. I need to speak to Mrs Smith personally.'

'Then you'd better come in.'

17

Margaret showed the policeman into the living room. 'Can I get you anything?' she asked.

'Just Mrs Smith,' he replied, quite obviously dismissing her.

Mags walked out of the room and left him standing there as she went upstairs. 'It's the police,' she said, knocking on Sharon's door. 'Some big-headed DI. He wants to see you.'

'Why?'

'Dunno. He wasn't very forthcoming. Didn't take to me at all. It's obvious he knows all about what happened in London. My suspension. Must have done his home-work.' She cursed the fact that the consequences of that day continued to follow her around.

'You'll come with me?'

'Of course.'

They both went downstairs to where DI Mahoney was pacing up and down the carpet. 'Mrs Smith,' he said to Sharon as they entered the room.

Sharon nodded.

'I need to speak with you… privately.' He gave Margaret a look.

'I want my sister to stay,' said Sharon.

Mahoney blew out a breath, not best pleased. 'She doesn't need to be here,' he said, not looking at Mags.

'I'll be the best judge of that,' said Sharon, her voice hard.

'Very well, if you insist.'

'I do. Please sit down.'

Mahoney took an armchair, Margaret and Sharon sat on the sofa. Margaret shut the door before she sat down.

'Mrs Smith,' said Mahoney, referring to a notebook he took from his pocket. 'First of all let me say how sorry I am for your loss. You and your family.' He gave Margaret another long look. 'But something new has come up in the course of our investigations.'

'What?' asked Sharon, perplexed.

'As you know,' Mahoney went on. 'We removed the car from the crash site and took it to be examined at our garage. Our technicians went over it and found something.'

'What?' Sharon again.

'The truck driver who witnessed the accident said that the car seemed to speed up instead of slow down on the hill. It seems the brakes were tampered with – the servo, so that the brake fluid leaked away. It was an inexact attempt at sabotage. The brakes could have failed just parking up outside the house. But unfortunately not.'

'Are you serious?' said Margaret, incredulously.

'I'm afraid so.'

'Wait a minute. Couldn't it have happened on

impact?' Mags looked at her sister, whose face was a picture of horror. 'Sorry Sharon, but this is crazy.'

The detective shook his head. 'No. Not possible. Our technicians are convinced. A team has been out to the crash site and they found brake fluid on the road.' Mahoney again turned to Sharon. 'I understand your husband was returning back from near the coast.'

Sharon nodded.

'A business meeting, I believe.'

Another nod.

'He was an accountant,' he said, looking again at his notebook.

'Yes.'

'Do you know where exactly the meeting was held?'

'No. A hotel or restaurant I believe, but I don't know where. Monty just said it was near the coast.'

'Isn't that rather strange? Out of office hours, in a public place?'

'I think they'd take a private room. I don't know. You know these businessmen, they do most of their important work over fancy three-course dinners. My husband's clients were sometimes very demanding,' said Sharon, her tone slightly imperious.

'How so?'

'Odd hours. Phone calls in the middle of the night. He didn't discuss his business with me.'

'But you don't know where this particular meeting was taking place?'

'She just said she didn't know,' interjected Margaret, glaring at the detective.

'That's another thing,' said Mahoney, ignoring her. 'I'm sorry to bring this up Mrs Smith, but when examined, your husband was over the legal limit for alcohol.'

Sharon started to cry.

Margaret held her hand and said. 'My sister's upset as you can see. Do we have to continue this now?'

'I'm fine,' said Sharon. 'Can I have some water?'

Margaret got to her feet. 'This is not the time,' she said to Mahoney, although she knew it was. She knew she would have done exactly the same thing in his shoes.

'I'm sorry,' he replied. 'But you know as well as I do...' He didn't finish the sentence.

Margaret nodded. 'Do you want anything?' she asked him, softening.

'A cup of tea would be great. I missed breakfast.'

'I'll only be a moment,' said Margaret and left the room, leaving Sharon staring numbly into space.

18

***

Margaret went into the kitchen, her mind racing after hearing what Mahoney had said. The kids were upstairs, but Frankie was sitting at the table with Roxie, talking quietly. 'What's up?' asked Roxie. 'You look awful.'

Margaret leant against the sink as she filled a glass with water. 'Christ,' she said. 'This is getting worse.'

'What's happened?' asked Frankie, her voice full of concern.

'This copper. Mahoney. Flash git. He reckons Monty's car was fixed.'

'How do you mean, fixed?' squealed Roxie, loudly.

'Ssshh, keep it down. Tampered with. The cops reckon the brakes were sabotaged.'

'Are you serious?' said Frankie, quietly.

'Yeah. Look, I'm going back. Make the sod a cuppa will you?'

'How did Sharon take it?' said Frankie, as she got up and filled the kettle.

'Not well. Would you? She was just getting a bit

stronger but I'm worried that this is going to put her right back where she started,' said Margaret, and left the room, glass in hand.

She went back to the living room where Mahoney and Sharon were sitting in silence, Sharon dabbing at her eyes with a tissue. She took the glass and gulped down half the water. 'Once again I'm sorry to be the bearer of bad news,' said Mahoney. 'But this is bound to alter the verdict at the inquest.'

'When will that be?' asked Margaret.

'Tomorrow. The coroner's court is in town.'

'We'll find it.'

'I'll call and let you know what time.'

'Thanks.'

Just then Frankie came in with tea, milk and sugar on a tray. Mahoney stood and was introduced to Frankie, who quickly left the room again, then sat back down and accepted a cup. 'We need to find out what happened and where,' he said to Sharon. 'Is there any way of finding exactly where your husband spent the evening? I'm sorry to keep on, but it's important.'

'I suppose Joyce might know,' she said.

'Joyce?' said Mahoney.

'Monty's secretary. Assistant. She's at home as far as I know. But she's as upset as the rest of us. She's been with Monty for years...' said Sharon, her voice trailing away.

Then Margaret remembered the jacket, wallet and phone that the uniformed sergeant had brought round the previous day. 'There were some things of Monty's that were recovered from the car. I've got them upstairs.'

'I know,' said Mahoney. 'I wonder if I could see them.'

'You didn't say,' said Sharon to her sister.

'I meant to,' said Margaret. 'I was going to tell you today. I just didn't want to upset you any more.'

'As if I could be,' said Sharon.

'I'll get them,' said Margaret.

'Shall I come with you?' asked Mahoney.

'No need. I won't be a minute.' She was gone before he could argue.

She ran up the stairs and collected the wallet from the drawer where she'd stashed it. She went through it fast. Cash, credit cards, a family photo of Sharon and the children, a couple of receipts, but nothing from the day he'd died. She stuffed everything back into the wallet and found the jacket in the wardrobe. It was empty except for one card tucked into the breast pocket. It was for the Crown Hotel, Lovedean, Hampshire and on the back was a mobile number scribbled in blue ink. She shoved it in her pocket and went back downstairs. At the sight of the familiar jacket Sharon started to cry. 'Sorry, love,' said Margaret, touching her on the shoulder, tenderly.

Mahoney took the jacket, the wallet and the phone. 'Can I search these?' he asked.

Sharon nodded.

He went though the pockets and the wallet carefully. 'Nothing here. I'll take the phone with me if I may,' he said. 'I'll have one of our technical blokes go through it, retrieve any information that may be germane, and get it back to you.'

'Germane?' said Margaret, her eyebrow raised,

He nodded, ignoring her sarcasm.

' So, is that all?' she said.

'For now. But I would like the number for Mr Smith's assistant.'

Sharon reeled it off, and he made a note in his book.

'Will you be there tomorrow? At the court I mean?' asked Margaret.

'I will,' said Mahoney, standing up to leave.

'We'll see you then, then. I think you'd better go now. Will you telephone if you find anything out today?'

'Of course.'

She showed him to the front door, and then went back to Sharon and hugged her tightly. She could only imagine what Mahoney's information would have done to her sister.

19

'We need to talk,' Margaret said to Sharon.

'I can't. Not now. I'm all confused. Monty was a good man. Who would do such a thing? Who would hurt our family like this?' her sister wailed.

'I know he was, love. And that's why it's so important we find out what happened.' said Margaret.

'Leave that to the police.'

'I am police. Well, you know what I mean.'

'No Mags. You'll get into trouble.'

'I already am, sis.'

'This is tiring me out, I can't think straight. I'm going upstairs to the kids. Try and get some sleep. I think I better take a pill.'

'Good idea,' said Margaret.

Sharon walked out of the room, shoulders slumped, and Margaret felt such a wave of pity as she looked at her inconsolable sister that she almost cried herself. Pull yourself together, she said to herself. No need for you to break down too. But instead she went out to her car and found a book of maps in the boot. Almost redundant now that the Boxster was fitted with Sat-Nav. She looked up Lovedean in the map and found it just off the A3 near the coast. She nodded, dumped the book back and went looking for Frankie and Roxie. 'Sharon's upstairs with the kids,' she said. 'The news has knocked her right back. She's going to try and sleep. Take a pill.'

'I still don't get it,' said Frankie, her face a mask.

'Me neither,' said Margaret. 'But I've got a clue.'

'What have you found?' said Roxie.

'I found a card in Monty's jacket for a hotel down south. Could be where he was that night.'

'So I don't get it?' came Roxie again.

'I'd like to know who he was with that night, and why? Because if he did have his car tampered with, that means our beloved brother-in-law was into some seri-ously dodgy shit and I intend to find out what it was.'

'Did you tell that copper about the business card?' Roxie asked.

Margaret shook her head.

'Why not?'

'Because he treated me like some twat without a brain. And because I wanted to do a little digging of my own first.'

'But he's old bill. I thought you lot stuck together.'

'Strictly speaking I'm not one of "you lot" at the moment. Anyway, I'm going to take a run down there. Shouldn't take more than an hour.'

'Less, if I drive,' said Roxie.

'You want to come?'

'Try and stop me. It's a nice day. Get the roof down

and away we go.'

'Frankie?' said Margaret.

'No. I'll stay here with Sharon. I'm too old for adventures. Anyway, if she takes a pill someone should be here if the kids wake up.'

'Course,' said Roxie. 'Never thought of that.'

'Just being an auntie,' came the smug reply.

'I'm one too.'

'And you'll have plenty of time to practise I hope. You two go. I think you're mad, and it will end in tears, but I know I can't stop you,' said Frankie warningly.

'It already has,' said Margaret. 'Come on Rox, if you're coming. No time to waste.'

20

———•———

Margaret went upstairs and got her jacket, and quickly popped her head in to check on Sharon and the children. All three were fast asleep in the double bed, and she crept away and down the stairs.

Roxie meanwhile was wearing a sheepskin jacket that she'd found hanging in the hall. 'She won't mind me borrowing this I'm sure,' she said as she slipped it on and admired herself in the mirror by the door. 'They didn't stint, did they,' she said. This is five hundred quid's worth if it's a penny.'

'Monty did well.'

'Maybe he was doing *too* well,' said Roxie. 'If what you said was right.'

Margaret just nodded in reply. She had her own ideas but didn't want to share them just yet – not even with Roxie.

They went out to Margaret's car, and Roxie demanded the keys. 'Are you sure?' said Margaret.

'Oh come on, you said I could,' said Roxie, in the same

cajoling tone that had always worked on the family when she was a little girl.

Mags smiled to herself but said, 'actually I didn't, and you're not insured.'

'So we break a few laws. Where's your sense of adventure girl?'

'Sense of adventure or not, I'm still a copper.'

'Who's been suspended through no fault of her own. Come on sis…'

Reluctantly Margaret handed over the car keys and Roxie jumped in and looked at the controls. 'Piece of cake,' she said. 'How do you get the top down?'

'Press that button.'

The soft top slid back smoothly and Roxie started the engine. 'Sweet,' she said as she gave it some revs.

'Come on, let's get going before you wake them upstairs.'

'Sorry,' said Roxie with a mischievous smile, as she slipped the gear lever into reverse and backed out of the drive.

'Turn left at the end,' said Margaret. 'The A3's a mile away.'

'Can't wait,' said Roxie, as she shifted into first gear and shot off down the road. 'A Thelma and Louise trip. What music have you got?'

Margaret hit the button for the CD changer and her favourite album began to play.

'Who's that?' said Roxie above the sound

'Cowboy Junkies.'

'Blimey. No wonder you're on suspension.'

'Funny.'

'So what happened? I heard you shot someone.'

'Dead right.'

'But not dead?'

'No,' said Mags, shortly.

'You'll be OK then. Super-cop will get through this.'

'Stop calling me that. Anyway, that Mahoney didn't seem to think so.'

'The copper? I had a peep when he left. A bit tasty eh?'

'I didn't notice.'

'He noticed you though. I saw the look he gave you.'

'Piss off.'

'Come on, admit it. He was a bit of all right.'

'If you say so,' said Margaret, forcing herself not to smile at her irrepressible sister.

'Come on Mags. Things can't be so bad that you don't notice a good-looking bloke.'

'You'd be amazed. My boss got shot. I shot an unarmed man. My job looks like it could be all over. I might be up in court. And now this. I've no time to be checking out the talent.'

'OK. Maybe things are that bad.'

Mags looked at her. 'Are you taking the piss?'

'No. As a matter of fact, I know how you feel.'

'You're doing all right, aren't you?' said Mags, perplexed.

'You'd be amazed. But I'll tell you another time. Just let me drive, OK.'

'OK.'

They hit the slip road for the A3 and Roxie let the car have its head. 'Nice,' she said, the wind whipping her hair round her face.

'You have heard of speed cameras haven't you?' said Margaret. 'I don't need a summons.'

'Bright yellow things on poles, like this one coming up,' Roxie laughed, but slowed down nevertheless. 'See sis, no problem,' as they passed it. 'Now who did you shoot?'

Margaret told her what had gone down, Utter's death and her shooting of an unarmed man. Instead of the shock she had expected, Roxie said. 'Shooting's great though isn't it. What a buzz.'

'What do you know about shooting?' asked Margaret.

More than I can tell you, thought Roxie, remembering Tony's body lying on the shop floor back in Spain. Wonder if they've found it yet. With the weather the way it had been, it would've gone off pretty quickly, and that would bring the neighbours nosing about. 'Loads,' she replied. 'When I was on the cruise ships after I first left England, we used to go into the Gulf of Mexico, stopped off in New Orleans. Before the hurricane of course. Smashing place. I cried when I saw what happened on TV. Had some great nights there. Met a bloke. A real cowboy. Pick-up truck, alligator skin boots, check shirt, the whole nine yards. Looked like that geezer who sang *Achy Breaky Heart*, remember him? A real hunk. Crazy about guns. Had a load of them back at his shack. Well, actually it was a penthouse. He had money. Took me out on the range. Shooting range that is. Taught me to shoot. Made me wet I can tell you. Then one weekend we flew up to Vegas, and we went out machine gun shooting in the desert. Blowing up cars and all sorts. Made me even wetter if you know what I mean. After that, we hardly left the room the rest of the time we were there,' said Roxie absent-mindedly, thinking back to those days.

'Yuck, little sis. I don't want to know – too much information,' said Mags.

'But fun,' said Roxie as she dropped a gear and over-took a truck.

'Slow down,' said Margaret. 'This can't be far from where Monty had the accident.'

'You want to look?'

'Someone should. I mean, someone who's not the police.'

'OK, but it's a bit morbid.'

'I'm feeling morbid.'

'That's why I wanted to get out of the house. It's grim in there.'

'What do you expect?'

'I know. Sorry. I didn't mean that. I was only little when Mum died but I remember how sad everyone was. It must have been as grim as this is.'

Worse, thought Margaret, but said nothing. After they drove through Petersfield, Roxie kept to the speed limit, and on the crest of a hill they saw police tape blowing in the breeze on the opposite side of the road. 'This must be it,' said Margaret. 'Pull over.'

21

Roxie bumped the Porsche up onto the verge and switched off the engine. Cars and lorries rushed by and shook the car. Margaret got out of the passenger side. 'Coming?' she asked.

'No. I'll just sit here and see if you've got any half-decent music in your collection.'

'Cheeky cow. I won't be long'

Margaret waited for another break in the traffic and ran across the dual carriageway. She climbed the verge that was rutted with tyre tracks from whatever vehicle had pulled Monty's car away from the scene, and the transporter that had taken the car to the police garage. The fence and hedge that had grown around it was broken and there were deep scars on the grass beyond. She jumped down through the gap, cursing her stupid decision to wear high-heeled boots and walked across the small field to the tree line. There she found a tree where the bark was ripped and torn. She stood for a moment, the only sounds coming from the whooshing of

Stop重

LEE MARTIN

the cars on the road behind her. Damn them, she thought. Whoever did this. She had never been particularly fond of Monty, but as her sisters always said, she had never been particularly fond of many people. That was one of the reasons she had joined the police. She had no pity for the people she had banged up, but sometimes she found solace in the care she could take of the victims.

And now her own sister was a widow and her niece and nephew had been left without a dad. Maybe she could help them find some peace of mind by discovering what had gone on the night that Monty had seemingly been sent to his death.

She lit a cigarette that she found in her pocket and swore there and then to do exactly what needed doing – whatever trouble it brought to her door. Turning, she made her way back to the road where she stamped out the cigarette butt and ran back to the car. 'Come on then,' she said to Roxy, who was listening to some godawful house music on the car radio. 'Let's go and see what we can see.'

22

When Margaret left the car, Roxie turned the music down, sat back, and let the sun warm her face. She had no desire to see the scene. Talking about shooting had brought back more memories. Memories of that time in America. She hadn't told Margaret the whole story. Far from it. More lies. It seemed her whole life had been a lie. She'd met the bloke all right. And he did have money. At first he'd told her it was a legacy – a trust fund, and she'd believed him. She'd been younger then, and more trusting of men. That was another problem. Men. She had always attracted the wrong sort, and been attracted to them in her turn. This one had been called Chase. And he *had* looked like the *Achy Breaky Heart* bloke. Tall, muscular, handsome, wearing a checked shirt cut to show his ripped arm muscles, he drove the biggest, fastest, most ostentatious red pick-up truck she'd ever seen. He'd picked her up in a bar in the French quarter of New Orleans one boiling hot night, when she was dizzy from the smell of exotic flowers and spicy gumbo coming from the restaurants on the street, combined with cigar smoke and the heady perfumes worn by the beautiful women packing the pavements. The sights and sounds combined with the lethal cocktails she'd been drinking since the boat docked made her head swim. But in a good way, so when handsome Chase sidled up, cut her out from the other crew members, and took her to another bar, darker, more scary, she didn't care.

Then, he took her for a drive through the back roads of Louisiana, speeding through the black night with the headlamps off, smoking dope, and occasionally stop-ping for a line of cocaine. Then back to the city to his penthouse in an apartment block by the river. More drinks, more drugs, then wild sex that lasted so long she literally missed the boat.

But Roxie didn't care. By then she was in love. There was cash everywhere, and she put it down to Chase's parents keeping him topped up. Chase took her out to a firing range and taught her how to shoot hand guns. Then there was the weekend in Vegas, where they'd almost got married in the Little Chapel by an Elvis impersonator – if they hadn't been kicked out for being coked-up – and the further lessons at the firing range, this time using automatic weapons. Roxie found a high in shooting a gun that she had only felt previously under the influence of class As.

Then one fine morning, Chase turned round, and said. 'I think it's about time we went to work.'

'I thought you didn't have to work,' she replied. 'Family money, and all that.'

'I kinda exaggerated that bit sweetness,' he said. 'It is

family money – in a manner of speaking. Just not *my* family, if you get my drift.'

She felt a cold hand on her heart. 'So what kind of work?' she asked.

'Honey, I rob banks.'

'Christ,' she said. 'For a minute there I thought you wanted me on the game.'

'The game?' he said, then fell in. 'What whore you out you mean?' He laughed long and loud. 'Baby girl,' he said, 'I'm a one-woman man, and I expect my girl to be a one-man woman. Though the way guys look at you, I'm sure we could make a dollar or two.'

'Chase, don't.'

'Sweetie, I'm only kidding. I would never do that to my lady. Now usually I work with a guy, but he got into a piece of local difficulty over a pool game that went all to hell, and he's doing ninety days on the farm for breaking a guy's skull with the thick end of his stick, so I need a driver. And I've seen the way you drive, so it looks like my search is over.'

'The truck?' she said.

'Hell no. Something a little less noteworthy. I'll fix that up. You game?'

'Sure,' said Roxie. 'When?' Simple as that. But she *was* in love.

Chase told her that there were two small, local banks that were ripe for the picking. Straight in, straight out, no violence, just show them his gun, and that was that. The bank's staff were ordered to just hand over the cash. No heroics. A sweet deal. He'd done it scores of times all over the country. Then he told her they'd move on out of New Orleans. Head down to Texas maybe, and live high for a while until they needed more cash, then the same again. His buddy would catch them up, or not. It was up to him.

When she told him of her family background he roared with laughter again. 'I knew I'd picked the right old lady,' he said.

So Roxie became a bank robber.

She was young and dumb, and Chase told her it would be easy. She believed him. 'Piece of cake,' she said, tilting her chin up and looking at him defiantly.

'Piece of cake,' echoed Chase. 'I like that. And you're the icing on my cake honey.'

23

The first job was at a branch of United Americas Bank, in a town outside New Orleans called St. Bernard. Chase had stolen a powerful, dark-coloured Chevrolet saloon which blended in with the traffic, plus a couple of sets of number plates that corresponded to the car. One week later they cruised into town during the quiet of a weekday lunchtime. Roxie was at the wheel, with a nine millimetre automatic tucked under her belt and Chase had exchanged his western clothes for a set of dark overalls, his long hair up under a woollen cap. He carried a pump action twelve-gauge shotgun in a workman's bag.

'Drop me off at the corner,' he said. 'Keep the engine running. When you see me go in, drive very slowly to the front of the bank and wait. I should be out within two minutes. I jump in the back, and Sweetie, we're gone.'

It all went according to plan. A parking space opened up in front of the building just as she arrived. The door to the bank burst open and Chase came tearing across the pavement, Roxie shoved the back door open, and he dived into the rear seat. She smashed her booted foot on the accelerator and the big car jumped away from the kerb with a scream of tires and smoke from the back wheels, up to the next set of lights which went green as if ordered to by a higher power. Roxie spun the car around the first corner and they were away out of town before the bank's alarm had a chance to alert anyone to the heist.

'Slow down,' said Chase from the back seat. 'Stay legal.'

'Did we get much?' asked Roxie.

'Enough to buy the finest dinner in The Big Easy, and a present for the best girl in the world,' said Chase as he looked through the back window for any sign of pursuit. 'Now take the next left, and let me change the plates on this old girl.'

He did just that, and they drove back to New Orleans, dumped the Chevy in the car park of a shopping mall, and took a bus home. 'No cabs,' said Chase. 'They'd surely remember your gorgeous face.'

That night they dined in style, booked into a grand hotel and made love for hours. The next day they bought new clothes and Chase took Roxie to a jewellery store, treating her to a three carat, square cut diamond ring. 'There's no need,' she protested. 'We could live for weeks on that money.'

'I promised you a gift,' said Chase. 'And I always keep my promises. Anyhow, there's plenty more cash lying round ready to be picked up.'

Roxie felt a cold hand on her heart again. She just hoped that he was right.

As Roxie had feared, the second robbery didn't go as smoothly. It was in a town called New Iberia, and although at first it seemed just as simple a job, it went wrong when the bank guard disobeyed instructions, pulled his gun, and Chase shot him. The sound of gunfire alerted a passing cop, and when Chase sprinted from the bank the police officer opened fire and hit him twice. He made the back seat of the Ford they were using this time for the getaway, but Chase was dying. Roxie took off again, but the cop was on her tail. They sped out onto the highway, but police cars were coming from all directions. Then they had the only stroke of luck of the day. Rain clouds had been gathering all morning and, as the pursuit progressed, the heavens opened. Roxie had never seen a storm like it before, even though she had spent time in the tropics on board the cruise ship. The rain was almost solid and the wipers could hardly cope, even at their fastest setting. 'Take any turning,' gasped Chase. 'Drop the car, take the money and get lost.'

'You need a hospital,' shouted Roxie above the roar of the water.

'I need an undertaker,' he said. 'Just do it babe. Go home, get your passport and head for Mexico. Take the truck. It's clean.'

Roxie looked over her shoulder. The back seat was awash with blood and Chase was deathly-white under his tan. He'd been right. His next stop was the mortuary. 'Do it babe,' he said. 'I'm going. I love you…' he said, as his voice disappeared in a gurgle of blood leaking from his mouth.

Roxie fishtailed off the main road, drove the car into a gap in the undergrowth and leant over the back seat but it was too late. Chase was dead, staring open eyed at the lining of the roof. She started to sob at the sight of him, but then her survival instincts kicked in. She knew there was nothing she could do for him, and this was no time for sentimentality. She was a Doyle, and her Doyle upbringing took over. She grabbed the money bag and dived out of the car, into a wall of rain which almost knocked her off her feet. There was no sign of the cops and she ran and ran until she found a bridge over a swollen river where she hid until the weather cleared and darkness came. She stayed there, shivering and soaked until sunrise. There was still no sign of a police presence, so she kept walking, hiding in the bushes by the side of the road if she heard the sound of an engine that might be cops. Eventually she came to a diner and gas station, used the facilities to make herself look more respectable, had breakfast, then charmed a truck driver into giving her a lift back to New Orleans. He was middle-aged and fat, and she thought he didn't offer much of a problem. But if he did, she still had her pistol under her jacket. Luckily for him, he turned out to be a perfect gentleman, and went out of his way to drop her off close to home – but not too close. The robbery was on the radio and TV news, but he didn't suspect the little English girl who'd lost her lift after an all night party, and needed to get back to the city. She headed back to the apartment, collected her stuff, counted the money – it was only a few thousand dollars, and hardly seemed worth getting killed for – took Chase's truck and did exactly what he'd said.

She got clean away and ended up in Mexico city, selling the truck for half its value to a kid who asked no questions. She quickly bought a ticket to Spain, and tried to forget him.

Sitting there by the side of the A3, it occurred to Roxie that she was constantly leaving dead boyfriends behind.

24

—⟫•⟪—

Roxie jumped when Margaret got into the car. 'Sorry,' she said. 'Miles away.'

'Is something wrong?' asked Margaret.

'Not really.'

'Not my business?'

'Don't be daft. Just things. What did you see over there? Anything useful?'

'No. Just the crash site. Not a nice thing, but I needed to see it.'

'Once a copper eh?'

'Something like that.'

Margaret took out the card from the hotel, leant over and punched the post code into the Sat-Nav. 'Used one of these before?' she asked.

'Course,' said Roxie. 'I live in Spain, not on Mars. We do have them there.'

'OK, clever clogs,' said Margaret.

'That's what we used to call you,' said Roxie. 'When we were kids.'

'Not very clever now, am I? No job prospects, no man. No kids.'

'There's always Mahoney,' said Roxie with a grin.

'Bollocks.'

'Anyway, you're not alone,' said Roxie. 'Not on the man and kids front anyway. Look at the four of us – only two kids between us.'

'Yeah. You would've thought Frankie would have had a brood by now. A natural mum.'

'She does have a brood. All of us. It's just as well really, you remember how much of a bastard Foster turned out to be, smacking her round and drinking all the time. Good job that marriage didn't last very long. Christ only knows what monsters any kids of his would have been.'

'You're right,' said Margaret. 'I could never work out what she saw in that arsehole.'

'You're not the only one. Shame she never found anyone else though. She's got so much love to give.'

'Enough of that. You'll have me in tears. Let's go.'

Roxie started up the car, waited for a gap in the traffic and headed off. 'So what's our story for the hotel?'

'Engagement dinner I reckon,' replied Margaret. 'Half a dozen girls out on the razz. Business women letting their hair down, lots of food and wine. We've heard that it's a decent place and we've got cash to spend. Course it might just be a B&B, but I doubt it. The card's all embossed and copper plate and I'm guessing the people that Monty worked for wouldn't slum it in some poxy venue. Just follow my lead. We'll busk it.'

'One problem though' said Roxie. 'Neither of us has a ring on.'

Mags sighed. 'Then keep your bloody hands in your pockets.'

'OK. Just one other thing. Your boots are covered in mud. Doesn't look too clever if you know what I mean. Especially if it *is* posh, and we're supposed to be,' said Roxie smugly.

'Yeah thanks sis. I've got some wet wipes in my bag so I'll clean them when we get there. Since when did you turn into the fashion police, anyway?'

'Just trying to help,' said Roxie with a giggle.

They drove down the A3 until the Sat-Nav directed them off to a roundabout under a flyover, and then onto b-roads until they passed Lovedean itself, a picturesque village that could have doubled as the location for some TV series set before World War 2. A mile or so later they arrived at a pair of large ornate gates which led onto a driveway of an imposing old house set in manicured lawns. 'I thought so,' said Margaret. 'A country house hotel. All the rage fifteen years ago.'

'Doesn't look too bad now,' said Roxie as she slid the car to a halt on a gravelled turnaround in front of the building.

Margaret jumped out and cleaned the mud off her boots, before the pair of them went up a short flight of stone steps and into the foyer of the hotel.

The interior was cool and plush, marble-floored with leather sofas dotted around, all with low tables in front of them. It was deserted at this time of day, apart from a young blonde behind the reception desk. Margaret led the way.

'Good morning,' said the blonde, whose name tag read 'Josie'.

'Good morning,' said Margaret. 'I wonder if you can help.'

'I'd be happy to.'

'We're looking for a venue for a dinner. An engagement party for my friend here. Old friends. All women.'

Roxie smiled, but remained silent.

'That certainly sounds like something we can help with,' said Josie, warmly. 'Were you looking for one of our private dining rooms?'

'That sounds perfect. We're a bit old for a night in a stretch limo wearing a veil covered in condoms, so we're looking for something a little discreet and classy, and we've heard good things about the hotel. In fact, some friends of ours were here – the night before last I think,' Margaret went on.

'Really,' Josie said, quizzically.

'Yes. A group of gentlemen who had a business meeting here recently.'

The blonde punched something into her computer,' and said. 'Oh, that would be the Haywood party. Regulars. Yes, they had a private room. Dinner for five.'

Gotcha, thought Margaret. It must be them. 'That's right. They were very complimentary of the food.'

'The chef will be pleased,' said the blonde. 'He came from The Savoy, you know.'

'Well that's it,' said Roxie. 'Sounds just right for my friends.'

'How many would there be?' asked the receptionist, smiling.

'Six or seven,' said Margaret. 'And of course we'll need rooms.'

'Excellent.'

'Could we see the private room?' said Margaret.

'I'm afraid the manager's not available at the moment, and I'm all on my own. If you could just wait for a few minutes…'

'Just for a second,' said Margaret. 'We're in a bit of a rush. Work, you know. We've got to get back to the city before the traffic hits.'

The blonde looked perplexed. 'Please,' said Roxie in a wheedling tone. 'It's so important to find the right ambience.'

'OK,' said the blonde. 'I'll have to be quick though.'

'Thank you,' said Roxie.

The blonde came out from behind her desk. 'It's upstairs,' she said, pointing at an imposing staircase. 'Then just down the corridor. There's a spectacular view of the river. It's all lit up at night, looks beautiful.'

'Lovely,' said Roxie, all smiles, warming to her role.

'Can I just use the loo?' said Margaret.

'Of course. There's one through there in the bar,' said the blonde indicating a door in the corner.

'I'll catch you up,' said Margaret.

'Top of the stairs, turn left, third on the right,' said the blonde, and headed for the staircase, Roxie in tow.

Margaret went to the door of the bar, opened it, and stood behind it for a moment whilst she waited for them to disappear. As soon as the coast was clear she headed back to the desk, spun the computer screen round and saw the booking for Haywood. No address, just a phone number. It wasn't a mobile number, so not the one on the card, and the notation 'paying by cash'.

She pulled a pen from her pocket and added the number to the one on the card, then swung the computer back and made her way up the stairs to the room where she was sure Monty had had his last meal.

After a brief look round, with Roxie showing the appropriate enthusiasm for the room, they returned to the foyer where Josie gave them menus and room prices – and Margaret gave her a false phone number. They left the building and went back to the car. 'What do you reckon?' asked Roxie.

'That must be it,' said Margaret. 'I got a number for Haywood, whoever he is. It's a London number.'

'Can you trace it?'

'I've still got some friends,' said Margaret. 'No problem. Let's go back, and I'll make some calls.'

25

―――――⟫・◦・⟪―――――

On the way back the two sisters stopped off for lunch in an Italian restaurant in Guildford. Roxie wanted to tell Margaret everything that she'd left behind in Spain but still wasn't sure how her sister would take it. She was a copper, after all. So instead, she asked. 'So what's the plan?' when they were seated at a quiet table by the window, a bottle of red wine between them.

'Like I said,' said Margaret. 'I've still got some friends. One in particular. He's an IT wizard.'

'Good looking?'

'Don't you ever think of anything else? No. He's like that scientist in *The Simpsons* – you know, the one with the stutter and Coke bottle glasses – and has unfortunate hygienic habits. Still after getting into my pants though.'

'Lucky you.'

'I'm going to get him to trace these two numbers for me.'

'Will he do it?'

'If I'm nice to him. Trouble is, Mahoney's got Monty's

BlackBerry. Christ knows what numbers are in it.'

'Did you have to give it to him?'

'I had no choice.'

'You didn't have a chance to check it out?'

'Didn't think it would matter. It was an accident, or so we thought. Then there's his office computer. They're bound to impound that, if there's any suspicion that Monty was murdered.'

'Do you think there is?' Roxie drew a sharp breath at the mention of murder.

'According to Mahoney. We'll find out for sure at the inquest tomorrow. Open verdict I reckon.'

'What about the funeral?'

'They should release the body all right. Then we can sort it out. You will stay, won't you?'

'I told you. Long as I'm needed. I want to help you find out what happened.'

'It could be dangerous though, Roxie. You know that, don't you?'

'I live for danger – I'm a Doyle, remember?'

After they'd finished their pasta they headed back to the house. Sharon and the children had gone out for a walk, so Frankie was the only one home.

'Anything?' she asked when the two sisters came in.

'Could be,' said Margaret. 'I'm going upstairs to make a call. How are they bearing up?'

'Not good,' replied her eldest sister. 'I thought it best for them to get out of the house – the phone never stops ringing and Sharon's getting more and more upset.'

'It's to be expected,' said Roxie. 'I'll hold the fort a bit. You go and have a sit down Frankie.'

'I'll go outside for a fag first. Don't like to smoke in the house.'

Margaret went upstairs to her room and sat on the bed. She thought about the coke in her shoe, but picked up her mobile instead and called a London number. 'Spike,' a man's voice answered.

'Hello Spike,' she said. 'How are you today?'

'The lovely Miss Doyle,' the voice said. 'What a pleasant surprise. But should I be talking to you?'

'Probably not.'

'So what can I do for you – aren't you off duty for the foreseeable? Don't tell me – is our date on at long last?'

'That depends...'

'I sense a favour being asked.'

'Maybe.'

'Spit it out. It can't be official, because I hear you've been a very naughty girl.'

'Don't piss about Spike. You know everything that's going on. Probably knew before I did that I was on suspension.'

'Probably, but you know me, I don't like to gossip,' he said, smarmily.

Mags said nothing but rolled her eyes.

'I need two numbers traced.'

'Why?'

'My brother-in-law died in a car crash two nights ago. It might not have been an accident.'

'Samantha Spade eh? A little private investigation to keep your hand in?'

'I just want to know what happened.'

'Guildford, was it?'

'What?'

'Guildford. You are in Guildford aren't you?'

Despite herself Margaret smiled. 'Clever boy.'

'State of the art. I can trace mobile phone calls anywhere in the world, anytime.'

'Makes me feel all warm inside.'

'And so you should. You'd be amazed how much the Home Office are prepared to spend on toys for me.'

'No I wouldn't.'

'Right.' Spike was suddenly all business. 'Give me the numbers and I'll call you back.' Obviously someone had interrupted him. She reeled them off, and with a hurried 'Bye,' he was gone.

She thought again about the drugs hidden in her shoe, and this time she decided to give them a go. So she did.

26

———⟫•⟪———

Just after Mags snorted the line, there was a knock on her door. 'Give us a minute,' she shouted, wiping her nose, and dropping a towel on top of the wrap of cocaine. Then, calling 'Come in,' Roxie stuck her head around the door. She had in her hands two cold beers.

'Fancy a drink?' she said.

'Sure,' said Margaret. 'Just the job.'

Roxie came in, shut the door behind her and sat on the edge of the bed. She passed one can to Margaret, and cracked her own.

Roxie looked at her and laughed out loud.

'What?' said Margaret.

'Your nostril.'

'What about it?'

'Take a look.'

Margaret went to the mirror on the wall. There was a residue of white powder on her top lip. 'Oh fuck,' she said, 'I look like Amy Winehouse.'

'Except you've got better hair – just. Is that what I

121

think it is?' asked Roxie. 'Or have you just been too liberal with the talcum powder?'

'I give in,' said Margaret. 'It's what you think it is.'

'Mags, I'm surprised at you,' Roxie said in a mock-accusatory tone.

'I know, I know.'

'And you a policewoman too.'

'Suspended policewoman to be exact,' Mags retorted to her sister.

'Got a line for me then?' said Roxie, cheekily.

'Roxie, you're my baby sister. I can't be giving you toot.'

'And all grown up. I worked the ships don't forget, and Spain. Those old crims almost live on the stuff. Plus don't forget all those weekends I went out clubbing, I practically existed on e's and coke.'

'Don't tell me any more! You can have a bit,' said Margaret. 'But mum would've killed me.'

'I've been thinking a lot about mum lately,' said Roxie, as Margaret carefully lifted the towel off the dressing table.

'Me too,' said Margaret. 'Right now, I'd've loved to be able to talk to her about what's happening. The job; now Monty.'

Roxie went to the table, cut out a line with Margaret's credit card, rolled the ten pound note next to it tighter, knelt, and snorted the drug. She drew in a sharp breath. 'Good stuff,' she said.

'Good dealer,' said Margaret. 'I cut him some slack a while ago, and now he lets me have the best for a knock-down price.'

'You must introduce us.'

'Maybe. Maybe later. Who knows when all of this will be over.'

Roxie sat on the bed again. 'Remember that party?' she asked, deep in thought.

'Which one?'

'My sixth birthday. The day mum collapsed.'

'I'll never forget it. How could I? Ambulance, and then the bad news.'

'Seems to me, it was the last day I was really happy.'

'Dolly, I'm so sad to hear that. But the same goes for me.'

'Jesus, that sucks,' said Roxie. 'Mum would have wanted us to live our lives.'

'I know.'

'Remember that bloke?'

'Which one?'

'Some hanger-on arsehole. One of those Z-list crims that used to hang around the house, always pissed. Asked you what you were going to do when you grew up.'

Margaret laughed. 'I remember.'

'You told him you were going to be a copper, and arrest people like him.'

'Yeah. Mum gave me a bollocking for that.'

'His face.'

'And I ended up doing just that, did you know? Not him personally, but some of the family.'

'You *didn't*.'

'Had no choice. Part of the job. They were testing me.'

'And you passed, I'm sure.'

'With flying colours. It wasn't a choice. I didn't want to be part of that world anymore.'

'Fuck 'em,' said Roxie. 'They soon vanished after mum went. Left us up shit creek.'

'Yeah, so much for brotherhood amongst the criminals. They couldn't wait to muscle in on her patch and leave us high and dry. And poor dad.'

'Maybe we should've realised this a bit more at the time, the pair of us. Instead of acting up like we did.'

'We weren't much help were we?' said Roxie.

'More of a hindrance.'

'But he had Frankie. She took over.'

'And look what he did to her. Knocking her about. And she took it just to save the rest of us, without a word.'

'I know,' said Roxie. 'Do you think I don't feel bad? We didn't know at the time. And we were only small. You know we can never repay Frankie for what she did for us.'

'God, oh why did mum have to go like that?' said Mags suddenly, feeling a rush of sadness at the thought of her mum, and the sister who bore so much to save her sisters.

'Dad never got over mum did he?'

'No. Never. Even with those other women.'

'And the booze – and the drugs.'

'Talking of drugs, can I do another line?'

'Help yourself,' said Margaret. 'But leave some for me.'

27

It didn't take long for Spike to get back to Margaret, and he wasn't pleased. 'Christ,' he said. 'What the hell kind of people was your brother-in-law mixing with?'

'I don't know. That's what I want to find out. So what's the problem?'

'Those numbers you gave me were both red flagged. I could get into all kinds of trouble if anyone asks why I was making enquiries.'

'Who are they then?'

'Thanks for your concern.'

'Spike, I know you. You don't leave any trail.'

'Maybe not. But you could've warned me,' Spike said, still sounding agitated.

'I thought it was bloody obvious if I was asking. I'm not using you like the Yellow Pages.'

'OK, OK – same old spiky Doyle. But that date's on, all right. You owe me one, after this.'

'When this is all over.'

Spike seemed to be placated by that. 'Right,' he said.

'The London number is for a couple of businesses with offices in Kensington. Haywood Properties and Antarctic Holdings.' he gave her the address. 'The mobile belongs to Roger Haywood himself, and right now he's at the office.'

'Brilliant,' said Margaret. 'I really do owe you one.'

'And I'll collect.'

Over my dead body, she thought. 'OK, Spike,' she said. 'But I'm going to be busy for the foreseeable.'

'I can wait.'

'And you're sure there'll be no comeback to you?'

'I'm not just a pretty face,' he said.

Not even that, she thought, but bit her tongue. 'Right,' she said. 'Thanks again. I might need some more help though. If you're up for it,' she said, forcing herself to speak flirtatiously.

'I think I can manage that.'

'Cheers then. See you.'

'You can count on that. See you gorgeous.'

* * *

In the office of Roger Haywood, on the top floor of a glass and steel monstrosity overlooking Kensington Gardens, the CEO of Haywood Properties and Antarctic Holdings was not a happy man. Nor were the two members of his staff who were standing in front of his desk. 'He's got our money and you killed him,' said Haywood. 'That wasn't very bright was it?' The flash of his steely blue eyes belied his calm tone.

'Not personally sir,' said the older of the pair, a sharply and expensively-suited man in his late thirties, with fair hair.

'I know you wouldn't get *your* hands dirty Peter,' said

Haywood. 'But it's still down to you.'

'It was only supposed to put the frighteners on him,' said the other man; younger, also immaculately dressed in a dark suit.

'Well I'm sure it did that,' said Haywood. 'It broke his bloody neck as far as I can make out.'

'So what do we do?' asked Peter.

'We get the money back of course. I know Smith was dipping into it. That's a given. We factor that into our profit margin. But what's ours is ours, and I want it under my control. Bloody accountants. They're more devious than a barrow load of monkeys. That secretary of his, I bet she knows where the bodies are buried. They always do. The wives don't know shit but the secretaries run the show. Give her a tug, and get the cash back. Then deal with her.'

'What happens if she doesn't play?' Peter asked.

'Then get bloody serious. Come on Peter, you're head of security and she's an old woman. You know which way the ball bounces. Now get out, the pair of you, and leave me in peace.'

The two men turned and left, closing the door gently behind them.

28

The inquest the next day was a solemn affair, but went pretty much as Margaret had anticipated. The sisters were all there as they'd left Peter and Susan in the charge of the neighbour again. The case was adjourned after DI Mahoney gave the details of the accident as he knew them, the truck driver who had seen Monty's car veer off the road gave his evidence, and the police expert, when questioned about the brakes on the Jaguar, could only say that there was a problem with the servo and that the loss of fluid had caused the crash. When the coroner asked if it was possible that the brakes had been tampered with on purpose, the expert would only answer, 'Yes sir.'

At that, the reporter from the *Guildford Star* hurriedly left the court.

It was also noted in court that Monty's alcohol level was over the legal limit.

Afterwards, Mahoney buttonholed Margaret and pulled her away from the family. 'We found the number of a hotel in Lovedean in Mr Smith's BlackBerry,' he said. 'We checked with the hotel and it appears that he attended a business and dinner meeting there on the night he died.'

Margaret just nodded. She'd been well trained in giving nothing away.

'Funny thing is, it seems we weren't the only people interested in that particular meeting.'

'Is that right?'

'Two young women were asking about a venue for an engagement party, and seemed to know all about the meeting held there two nights earlier.'

'An engagement, that's a happy occasion, so I hear. I hope they have a good time,' said Mags, sweetly.

'Funnily enough the contact number they left was false, and the one asking all the questions fitted your description perfectly. And the other could be your sister.' He nodded over in Roxie's direction. 'Unfortunately the CCTV was on the blink, otherwise that could have been a very interesting bit of viewing.'

'Fancy that,' Margaret started to say, but was cut off by Mahoney.

'Don't piss me about Miss Doyle.'

'*Sergeant* Doyle.'

'Not at the moment, and never again if you interfere in a police investigation.'

'You've got me bang to rights *Inspector*.'

'Listen. I know this is a bad time for you and your family, so I'm prepared to overlook the matter. But tell me, and tell me the truth. Is there anything else you're keeping from me?' He looked Margaret square in the eye.

Margaret shook her head and hoped she didn't look flustered.

'I hope that's right. Now we've got a warrant to search Mr Smith's office. I don't want to bother Mrs Smith further, so could you get the keys and let us in. We're not going to ransack the place. It'll just be me and a DC. We'd like to do it as soon as possible please.'

'This afternoon?'

'If you could. And we've issued production orders on his bank accounts.'

'You're being thorough.'

'Of course. And listen, I had a word with a mate of mine in the Met. He says you're good people. I know your mum's reputation, of course. But you're a hard worker on the force, so I hear.'

'I'm flattered,' she said sarcastically.

Mahoney smiled. 'But no more messing about, right?'

Margaret didn't know whether to cross her fingers behind her back as she nodded in reply.

'Three o'clock do you this afternoon?' asked Mahoney.

'Yes. I'll meet you there.'

Mahoney nodded.

'I'd like to bring one of my other sisters.'

'Good idea. A witness is always handy. We want to do this by the book.'

'Three o'clock then,' said Margaret, and they parted on the steps of the coroner's court. She found herself watching him leave, noticing his tight arse in a fitted suit that looked Italian. Christ, she said to herself. You've got enough on your plate. Get it together. The last thing you need is to start wetting your knickers over some stuck up DI.

131

29

Back at the house, Margaret told the others about the warrant for Monty's office.

'This is horrible,' said Sharon. 'Do I have to be there?'

'No,' said Margaret. 'I'm going. And Roxie, I want you to come with me.'

'Why?'

'We need a witness. This has all got to be above board.'

'Fair enough. And I get to meet the lovely Mahoney in the flesh at last. I think he's got a thing for our Mags.'

'Roxie!' Margaret warned her.

'Just a joke,' said Roxie. 'We can still make jokes can't we? Or is it against the rules now?'

'Course we can,' said Sharon.

'I didn't mean…' said Roxie.

'I know love,' said Sharon. 'I'm just sorry to involve all of you. But I couldn't do it alone.'

'You're not alone,' said Frankie. 'And never will be.'

'Sorry Roxie,' said Margaret. 'I'm a bit stressed out

today. We got sussed out.'

'Do what?'

'Our little trip to Lovedean. The meeting was in Monty's BlackBerry. The local cops made a visit. They heard that two women were making enquiries. They got descriptions from that blonde in reception no doubt. Mahoney worked it out that it was us. I got a slap on the wrist and a warning off.'

'My, my,' said Roxie. 'Naughty us.'

'That's what I said. Which reminds me. I need to go to London tomorrow.'

'Why?' asked Sharon.

'A few things I need to do. Get some fresh clothes for one.'

'I'm coming too,' said Roxie. 'OK?'

'If you want.'

'Yeah, I left Spain in a hurry and I'm running out of fresh gear. A quick trip to Topshop will do me right.'

* * *

Margaret and Roxie arrived at the building that housed Monty's office just before three. It was a faceless modern building, split into units overlooking the river. Margaret parked up in front, and a few minutes later a dark saloon drifted into the car park. Mahoney and his DC got out.

Margaret and Roxie left the Porsche and joined them. After a brief introduction Mahoney produced his warrant. 'Got the keys?' he asked Mags.

'Right here,' said Margaret, taking the bunch from her handbag.

'Let's go then.'

The foyer of the building was empty, and no one was at the reception desk. 'Good security,' said the DC.

'Monty's office is on the top floor, Sharon said,' said Margaret. 'Unit twenty.'

They took the lift to the top, and walked down a short, empty corridor with doors on both sides. 'Quiet,' said the DC, who was the type of man who couldn't not state the obvious.

Nobody replied.

The corridor branched off to the left and unit twenty faced them. The door was ajar.

'Shit,' said Mahoney. Then, 'stay back,' to the two women, as he and the DC approached the door. The lock had been forced. 'Police,' he said loudly as he pushed the door open.

Inside, the office was empty and had been ransacked. Papers were everywhere, filing cabinets and desk drawers open. On the top of one of the desks was a computer with its insides scattered around.

The DC pulled on a pair of surgeon's gloves and went to it. 'Hard drives gone, Skip,' he said.

Mahoney turned to Margaret. 'If you had anything to do with this…'

Margaret held up the keys. 'I wouldn't need to break in. And it pisses me off that you'd think I did.'

'Who else works here?' asked Mahoney. 'He didn't work alone did he?'

'His secretary,' said Margaret. 'Joyce. She's been with him for years. She's nearly sixty. She wouldn't…'

'So where is she?'

'We told her to take time off. Frankie spoke to her. She came round yesterday. She's like part of the family. And she has a set of keys too.'

'We'll have to check with her. And I'm sorry I

suggested you did this. But it certainly looks like someone didn't want us to know Mr Smith's business.'

'I wonder who?' said Margaret.

'We'll find out.' Then to the DC. 'I want Scene of Crime in here right away. Secure the door and stay here until they arrive.'

The DC nodded and got out his mobile, calling in the Scene of Crime units.

Mahoney turned to Margaret. 'There's nothing you can do here,' he said. I'd like the secretary's address. I need to speak to her.'

'I don't know it,' Mags told him. She saw the look on Roxie's face out of the corner of her eye but remained impassive.

'Does Mrs Smith have it?'

'Naturally.'

He gave her his card. 'Please call me when you get back, and let me have it.'

'Of course,' said Margaret, and the two women left.

'Masterful, isn't he?' said Roxie as they went back to the car. 'A real man. But what was all that about not knowing Joyce's address, you liar?'

Margaret didn't answer. She had other things on her mind.

30

When the sisters got back to Sharon's she was with the children watching TV. Margaret and Roxie took Frankie in to the kitchen and told her what they had found at Monty's office. 'Christ,' she said. 'What the hell is going on?'

Margaret shrugged. 'It looks like Monty was involved with some very bad people. This is not good. Not good at all.'

'What sort of bad people?' asked Frankie, looking pale and nervous.

'That's what I intend to find out.'

'You should leave it to the police.'

'I am police. And this is my family. I need to speak to Joyce. Remind me of her number, love.'

'What about Mahoney?' said Roxie. 'You lied about not knowing Joyce's address but he can easily find it in Monty's stuff.'

'That's true, but I want to talk to her first. See what she knows. She was Monty's secretary after all – she'll know what was going on in that office.'

Frankie got out her address book and pointed to numbers for a land line and a mobile. Margaret took out her phone and tried both. 'The land line's engaged and the mobile's off,' she said. 'It's only five minutes to hers in the car. I'm going to go round.'

'Do you want me to come?' asked Roxie.

'No. You stay here. Tell Sharon about the office. This is only going to upset her again, so it's better if you're both here.'

She grabbed her keys and went out to the car. Joyce's house was closer to the centre of town. She put the address in her Sat-Nav and soon pulled up in front of a two up, two down end of terrace. She remembered it from giving Joyce a lift home on one of the few occasions the family had a big party. She parked outside, pushed open the front gate and went up the path. There was a light on in the hall, but no answer when she pushed the bell. Mags started to get a bad feeling. Joyce lived alone, had few visitors and was frugal, not one to waste electricity. She walked round the front of the house to the side gate when there was a rustling in the hedge and she jumped. 'Christ,' she said, 'bleeding hell kitty, you gave me a fright,' as Joyce's big, old grey Persian cat emerged from its hiding place. Margaret bent down to pet the animal, who she remembered was called Thomas. Joyce loved the cat like it was her own child. In a way, it was. 'You're all wet,' she said. Her heart started to pound with adrenaline.

The gate was on the latch so she pushed it open and went up the narrow path at the side of the house, followed by Thomas, mewing loudly.

The back door into the kitchen was closed, but unlocked, and Margaret knew that something was badly wrong. Joyce was a glutton for security, being a middle-aged woman living alone. Gingerly, she pushed open the door and called out Joyce's name. No answer. The kitchen was scrupulously tidy and Thomas's water and food bowl were empty on the floor with traces of dried food in one. Joyce would never have left the cat like that. Thomas slithered between Margaret's legs and started to miaow. 'Shh,' she said, then grabbed his water bowl, filled it, and placed it in front of him. He immediately shut up and started lapping at the liquid.

Margaret went into the hall. The living room was tidy but empty also. The phone sat on a side table, the receiver off the hook, the machine giving off a high pitched whine that made her wince.. Holding her jacket sleeve over her fingers, she replaced the instrument and the place was suddenly deadly silent.

She climbed the stairs and went into the back bedroom. Empty. The bathroom, the same. The front bedroom was Joyce's, and she gingerly pushed open the door. The curtains were drawn and the room was in darkness. Margaret fumbled for the light switch and as the bulb lit she saw Joyce lying on her bed. She blinked at the scene that lay before her, not quite believing her own eyes. Joyce was on her back, fully clothed. Her eyes were open and looking up at the ceiling and the pillow where her head was resting was a rusty brown colour. It appeared that she had a second mouth beneath her chin where someone had cut her throat from ear to ear. The only sound in the room was the buzzing of the flies circling the corpse on the bed.

31

Margaret didn't venture any further into the room. She knew a dead body when she saw one, and didn't want to disturb anything. She stood for a moment outside the room, dry eyed, although she felt a terrible sorrow for this harmless woman who had her life ended so brutally. Her police instincts kicked in and she cocked her head, listening carefully but all she could hear was the sound of traffic outside. The house was deathly silent and it was obvious that Joyce's killer was long gone. She went back downstairs to the kitchen where Thomas was still prowling hungrily about, picked up the protesting animal and took him into the tiny back garden. She hunted in her handbag for Mahoney's card, opened her phone and called his number.

'Mahoney,' he answered.

'It's Margaret Doyle,' she said. 'I'm at Joyce's house. Monty Smith's secretary.'

'I thought you were going to call me with her address...'

141

'I was,' she cut him off. 'I just wanted to see her for a minute. Tell her about what happened at Monty's office. Look, you'd better get over here, sharpish. Bring some uniforms and your SOCO team.' She reeled off the address.

'Why?' he asked.

'She's dead. Been murdered.'

'*What?*' came the exclamation at the other end of the phone.

'You heard. Are you coming?'

'Of course. Stay where you are.'

'I'm not going anywhere.' And she snapped her phone shut.

Thomas was still rubbing himself on her legs and distracting her thoughts, so she went back into the kitchen, opened the fridge door with a tea towel and saw a half full tin of cat food. She took it out, grabbed a saucer from the dresser, went back out, shutting the door behind her, and took both to the back of the garden where she emptied the tin onto the saucer and Thomas dived in. 'That'll keep you quiet,' she said aloud and went out to the street to wait for Mahoney and his crew. She found her cigarettes and lighter in the bottom of the bag and lit up, the nicotine helping to quell the growing panic that was rising in her. Who the fuck would have done this to Joyce?

She heard sirens long before Mahoney's car, and two squad cars sped into the street. With a sigh she dropped the cigarette butt onto the pavement and ground it out with the sole of her boot. 'Here we go,' she said to herself. 'What the hell did we all do to deserve this?'

32

Mahoney's car skidded to a halt in front of Margaret's Porsche, his ever-present DC at the wheel, and he was out of the passenger door almost before it stopped. 'What the fuck have you got into now?' he demanded.

'Language, sergeant,' said Margaret, coolly. 'Your public are watching,' she gestured to a couple of passers-by who were rubber-necking the scene.

'Come here,' said Mahoney, grabbing her arm and tugging her through the gate into the shelter of the hedge.

'Get off me,' said Margaret, shaking his hand off her. 'I'm not one of your suspects.'

'You might be,' he said.

'Don't be stupid. I rang you, remember?'

'Call me stupid again and I'll nick you.'

'What for?'

'I'll think of something.'

Meanwhile, the DC had joined them, and the uniforms were gathered outside on the pavement.

'Where is she?' asked Mahoney.

'Upstairs, front bedroom.'

'If you've contaminated my crime scene...' Mahoney didn't finish.

'I fed the cat, went upstairs, didn't touch anything. I'm a copper, I do know what to do.'

Mahoney made no comment at this. Instead he turned to the DC and said. 'Jacko, get upstairs, take a squint. Make sure there *is* a body.'

Margaret let out a snort as the DC pulled on another pair of latex gloves and went inside. 'You lot,' said Mahoney to the uniforms. 'Clear the area, and keep it clear. Tape it off.'

'So you do believe me,' said Margaret.

'Of course. You are police after all. Sort of. But you were the one being stupid. Going in there alone, no backup, *and* unarmed.'

'They took my gun away. Remember? Plus, I didn't think I was walking into a murder scene, did I?' said Margaret. But he was right. She had been foolish and regretted leaving her guns back in Battersea. Another reason for a trip home as soon as possible. Clean knickers, clean guns and more coke.

'Come on,' said Mahoney, and he led the way round the side of the house.

The DC was back before they reached the kitchen door. 'There's the body of a woman on the bed upstairs,' he said.

'Her name was Joyce Smart,' said Margaret.

'We'll wait for a relative to identify her,' said Mahoney.

'She has no relatives. Sharon's family were her family,

she always said, apart from Thomas.' said Margaret. For the first time she felt a lump in her throat and a tear in her eye, but she swallowed the lump back, and shook her head angrily.

'Thomas?' said Mahoney.

'The cat.'

'The one you fed.'

Margaret nodded. 'He was starving.'

'Lucky the doors were all shut or pussy would've been snacking on mum by now,' said the DC.

'She was a friend,' said Margaret, shooting daggers at him.

'Sorry,' said the DC. 'But it's happened before. You must've seen it.'

Margaret just glared at him, icily.

'Anyway, from first sight it looks like it was a straight killing. She's fully dressed. I don't think there was any fiddling about done. Mind you she was getting on. Not that *that's* ever stopped anyone.'

Margaret moved forward, grabbed the DC's hand and twisted his little finger back until she felt the tendons about to snap. He screamed and went down on one knee. 'I said she was a friend,' she hissed. 'Have some fucking respect or I'll break this like a matchstick.'

'Leave him,' roared Mahoney.

'Now apologise,' said Margaret, putting on more pressure.

'Sorry! Sorry!' said the DC in a high pitched voice.

Margaret let him go, and when he looked up he had tears in his eyes. 'Jacko. Get outside and wait for SOCO. And keep your big mouth shut,' said Mahoney.

When Jacko had gone, Mahoney said, 'technically, that

was assault of a police officer.'

'Think he'll press charges?' asked Margaret.

'What? And admit a woman made him nearly wet his Y-fronts? I don't think so. But watch him. I think you've made an enemy there.'

'Not the first,' said Margaret.

'I bet.'

33

———⊰•⊱———

Mags and Mahoney were interrupted when the SOCO team arrived and Margaret said. 'Do you need me anymore? I should get back and break the bad news.'

'That won't be easy, after everything else,' said Mahoney.

'Tell me about it. There seems to be nothing else lately,' said Margaret, shaking her head.

'It's a hell of a mess, I'll give you that.'

'You can say that again. Well, do you need anything more?' she said, looking at him directly.

'Not right now. But we'll need a statement and I'll want to talk to you again today.'

'Fair enough.'

'Do you fancy meeting for a drink tonight?'

'Tonight? Are you asking me on a date, Mahoney?'

'Don't push your luck', he said, smiling slightly now. 'But we should talk – away from your family.'

'Can't we do that down at the station?'

'Yes, but I can think of better places to be. What about

The George down by the river? Know it?'

'Sure, I know it. Will you be able to get away though, aren't you in the middle of the case?'

'It's police business and it will only be for an hour or so. And we *do* need to talk.'

'OK. What time?'

He looked at his watch. 'Say six?'

'Six it is.'

'What about the cat?' asked Mahoney.

'Oh Christ. I forgot about him. I better take him, you lot trampling about will frighten him to death.'

Margaret and Mahoney went back into the garden and found Thomas glaring at one of the SOCOs. 'It's all right,' said Margaret. 'He won't bite.'

'That's not my experience,' said the man, eyeballing the cat as it arched its back and hissed at him.

'I'll take him.'

'And you are?'

'It's OK,' Mahoney interrupted. 'She's family.'

The SOCO shrugged and Margaret picked up Thomas, who struggled for a second, then settled down in her arms. 'Later,' she said to Mahoney and took the cat out to her car. On the way she saw Jacko, who gave her another look that could kill. She put Thomas inside the Porsche and drove back to Sharon's, dreading what was to come.

Once back at the house, she left Thomas locked inside her car, hoping that he wouldn't tear her upholstery to shreds, and went to the kitchen where her three sisters were sitting around the table. Frankie saw the look on her face as soon as she walked in. 'What now?' she asked.

'This is not easy,' said Margaret slumping into an empty chair.

'What? Just spit it out sis,' said Frankie again.

'It's Joyce,' replied Margaret. 'She's dead.'

The colour left the faces of the other three. 'Are you serious?' said Roxie.

'It's not something I'd joke about.'

'How?' Sharon asked.

'Murdered. In her bedroom.'

'When?'

'Dunno. That's for the experts. By the look of her, maybe last night.'

Sharon moaned, got up, and slumped down deeply in her chair. 'How the hell am I going to tell the children? They loved her like a grandmother.'

Margaret sighed deeply. 'I don't know love. This is just about as bad as I've ever seen it.'

'What the hell is going on?' said Roxie, suddenly seeming very young and very scared.

34

Margaret literally slapped herself on the forehead. 'Christ,' she said. 'You're right. What am I thinking of?' Quickly, she grabbed her phone from her handbag and called Mahoney again. 'Mahoney,' she said, when he answered. 'I think we need some protection at the house, after all that's happened.'

'Go to the front door,' he said.

She did as she was told. Outside the house was a blue Mondeo with two up in the front. 'See them,' said Mahoney.

'I see them.'

'24/7 until this is over,' he said. 'But I think perhaps Mrs Smith and the children would be safer somewhere else. Is there anywhere they can stay?'

'I suppose. Do you think they're in danger?'

'*You* obviously do.'

'Yeah. Sorry. Just thinking aloud. There's Frankie's house, they could go there.'

'I was thinking about somewhere out of town,'

he answered.

'You're right. I don't know what's the matter with me.'

'We do have safe houses.'

'They're always horrible. At least they are if they're anything like the Met's.'

'Budget. It was hard enough getting manpower to baby-sit you lot, believe me.'

'I do. And thanks,' said Margaret, a note of gratitude entering her voice.

'Listen, I've got to go,' he said. 'Duty calls. See you later?'

'Sure. Bye.' She closed her phone, waved at the two coppers and went back inside.

'We've got minders,' she said to her sisters. 'For the duration. But Mahoney thinks Sharon and the kids should get away. Somewhere safe.'

'We *are* in danger,' said Sharon, looking horrified. 'My God.'

'We don't know it's anything to do with Monty's death,' interjected Frankie.

'No, we don't know for certain, but we have to be careful. Why would someone kill Joyce?' She turned again to Sharon. 'Calm down love,' said Margaret. 'A safe house might be for the best. How about Monty's mum's?'

'She's not well, you know that. That's why she's not here.'

'Might do her good to see you though.'

'I suppose. But what about the funeral?'

'Funerals,' said Frankie. 'There's no one to take care of Joyce's. We owe her.'

'God, yes,' said Margaret.

'We'll have a double funeral,' said Sharon.

'It might take time for them to release both bodies,' said Margaret.

Silence fell in the room as the four women took in the magnitude of what had happened.

Finally Roxie broke the silence. 'You're getting pally with Mahoney,' she said to Margaret.

'Police business,' replied Margaret. 'And I'm meeting him later.'

'What for?'

'Information. He's got it, we need it. Plus I've got to give a statement about finding Joyce. We're going for a drink.'

'Told you,' said Roxie. 'Told you they'd get friendly.'

'Do be quiet,' said Margaret. 'He's useful. And he has got us our protection.'

'What happened to Thomas?' Frankie asked suddenly.

'Oh Christ,' said Margaret. 'He's in the car. Probably tearing my upholstery to shreds. I couldn't leave him with all those hairy-arsed coppers milling about at Joyce's. He'd have done a runner. And we've lost too much already.'

'He can stay with us,' said Sharon. 'The kids always wanted a pet and it might take their minds off what's happening. And Joyce loved that moggy. We owe it to her. When will we have to move and where will we go?'

'I don't know when, but we should find something fast. There's safe houses,' said Margaret. 'If nothing else.'

'I'll call Monty's mum. You might be right. Do us all a power of good to get away.'

'That's my girl,' said Margaret, pleased that Sharon had finally started to come out of her dark depression, but still her mind was fixed on the sight of Joyce on her bed. Who would have done such a thing – and would they target her family next?

35

In fact, Thomas was curled up fast asleep on the driver's seat when Margaret went to fetch him. On the way back to the house she'd stopped at Tesco and bought food, kitty litter, a tray and food bowls for the animal. Bleeding hell she thought, this moggy's going to cost us a fortune – all the while knowing that she would never have left him, for Joyce's sake. She smiled at the two coppers still guarding the place, grabbed Thomas and took him inside. Peter and Susan had come downstairs and were delighted to see the cat, immediately fussing around him. 'What did you tell them?' Margaret whispered to Sharon. 'About Joyce I mean.'

'That Aunty Joyce has gone away for a bit. I didn't want any more tears before bedtime.'

'Best thing,' said Margaret.

At half five Margaret was ready for her meet with Mahoney. 'Have fun,' grinned Roxie as she left. 'Don't do anything I wouldn't.'

'Leave it out,' said Margaret, smiling in spite of herself.

'We still on for London tomorrow?'

'That's right,' said Mags. 'I need to pick some stuff up from the flat first.'

'Well don't be late back then, we should get going early'

'A drink,' sighed Margaret, 'that's all it is. Intelligence gathering. I'll be back before you know it.'

Roxie just waved, cheekily.

Mahoney was already at the pub when Margaret parked up, sitting outside at a table by the water's edge – a pint in front of him and a cigarette burning between his fingers. 'Didn't know you smoked,' said Margaret as she joined him at the wooden table.

'On and off. I'm just a social smoker. What are you drinking?'

'White wine,' she replied, and he stubbed out the cigarette and went into the pub.

When he got back and she had her drink, he said. 'Who'd've guessed it would happen. Can't even have a fag at the bar these days.'

'Not like the old days in the CID,' said Margaret. 'Smoke so thick you couldn't see across the room.'

'Happy days.'

'You don't look happy.'

'I'm not. This is a major case now. DCI involved. Super on the prowl. All the way up to the Chief Constable. We don't have that many murders in Guildford. Not this kind anyway. Some stupid kid with a knife stabs another stupid kid in a row over a DVD, and the little sod bleeds to death. Or some fisty husband going too far. Nothing like this. I'm no longer in charge. Just another face in the crowd from now on.'

'I doubt you'd ever be just a face in the crowd Mahoney.'

'Michael. Mike. And are you flirting with me?'

'Don't know. It's been ages since I've had a good flirt.'

'Me too,' he said, looking at her with a half smile.

'No Mrs Mike then?'

'No. Nor likely to be. No girlfriend. In fact I've only been in Guildford for a few months. Transferred from Aldershot.'

'That must have been fun. All that time busting squaddies.'

'That's about right.'

Margaret decided to get down to business. They were getting off the subject, pleasant though it was. 'When do you want my statement?' she asked. 'About finding Joyce.'

'Tomorrow morning. I've got an early meet with the DCI. Just passing stuff on so it should be over by nine.'

'Nine it is.'

'You know where the station is?'

'What do you think?' she said. 'Okay, enough small talk, let's get down to it. Tell me. Who's Haywood?'

Mahoney looked surprised and lit another cigarette before answering her question. 'What do you know about him?'

'Nothing. Just a name. And what about Antarctic Investments?'

'You have been doing your homework. Why do you want to know all this?'

'I'm a copper, remember? Just names to me too.'

'I'm interested. Fancy something to eat? There's a decent Chinese by the bridge.'

'Why not? I've got nothing else to do.'

'I've heard more enthusiasm, but never mind. Drink up then, and we'll go.'

36

—⊳•⊲—

Once seated in the restaurant with a bottle of wine and food ordered, Mahoney turned to Mags. 'You're determined to stick your nose into this aren't you? Nothing I can say will convince you?'

'Wouldn't you? Considering what's happened.'

'Probably. But you don't know what you're getting into.'

'Do you?'

'I shouldn't be telling you anything. You're on suspension. And you're too close to this case.'

'Come on Mahoney. Shit or get off the pot.'

'It's Mike, and you coppers from the Met certainly have a turn of phrase.'

'You ain't heard nothing yet. Come on, Mike. You know I'll find out one way or another so let's just get on with it shall we? The only thing I want to know is who wants to hurt my family like this?'

'So I imagine. OK, it's early days yet and all we have to go on is Mr Smith's palm top and a load of papers strewn around his office. I've got a DC on them, but so far they seem just to refer to the tax returns of half of Guildford's wealthy self employed. Architects, actors, singers, you know the sort.'

'I can't see a local architects cutting Joyce's throat over some overpaid tax, can you?'

He shook his head as the waiter delivered their starters. 'No. How long had Mr Smith been in business here?'

'Fifteen years, give or take.'

'Nice house, nice cars, kids at private school. He didn't get that sort of lifestyle sorting out punters earning the average wage did he?'

'I never thought about it.'

'Didn't you?'

'No. Straight up. Monty was dedicated to his family as far as I knew. And besides I was up in London. I visited for birthdays and sometimes Christmas, but I had a different kind of life from them. You know what it's like in CID. You're married to the job.'

'Someone's going to need to talk to your sister soon.'

'She thought she might take the kids to Monty's mother's place for a bit.'

'Where's that?'

'Norfolk.'

'Good idea, but she'll need to be interviewed first.'

'Take it easy with her, will you? She's vulnerable.'

'Might not be me. Female officer probably. We're not totally heartless.'

'No, you're not.'

They dug into the food and the evening passed effortlessly.

When they were finishing their after-dinner coffees, Margaret said, 'Listen, I'm going up to London tomorrow after I've given you my statement. I'll be honest. I'm going to do some digging around.'

Mahoney shook his head. 'I don't like it, but I suppose I can't stop you.'

'No you can't. You're lucky that I even told you that.'

'Just promise me you'll be careful, and if you turn anything up please ring me immediately,' said Mahoney, looking worried.

'So you do have some faith in me?'

'That's right. But what I've heard about you tells me you just might pull something out of the bag.'

'Which wouldn't do your career any harm if I did – and happened to tell you all about it. But remember Mike, one hand washes the other. A favour for a favour.'

'You can trust me, I hope you know that.'

'Now, it's been a lovely evening. Especially after what I saw today. But it's time for bed.'

Mahoney raised an eyebrow.

'Alone. Do you want to split the bill?'

'No, this is on me. You can pay next time.'

'If there is a next time,' she said, raising one eyebrow.

'Here's hoping then,' he said, and gestured to the waiter.

'I'll leave you to it then,' said Margaret. 'See you in the morning.'

'I'll look forward to it.'

Margaret got up, collected her things and shook his hand. 'Drive carefully,' he said. 'And remember what I said, these people don't care who they hurt,' he said as she turned to leave.

'Don't worry about me,' said Margaret, 'I'm a Doyle, and we look after our own.'

37

When Margaret got back to the house, a different car with two passengers was parked across the street. She nodded to the new police guards and went inside, where Roxie was waiting up for her, watching TV in the living room. 'Dirty stop out,' she said by way of a greeting.

'Are you my mother now?' asked Margaret.

'More like Frankie. Mum never had a chance to wait up for us, did she?'

'Sorry love, I didn't think.'

'Don't matter,' said Roxie, brightening up. 'So, how did your date go?'

'It wasn't a date,' said her sister, but avoiding her eyes by making a show of hanging up her coat and rustling through her bag.

'Just a drink, yeah?' She looked at her watch. 'So what time do you call this?'

Margaret laughed at her mock-serious tone, and impulsively went over and embraced her sister.

'Thought I'd wait up for you,' said Roxie. 'London, tomorrow. Right?'

Margaret nodded.

'I'll kip on the sofa. Don't want to disturb Frankie by going back to hers.'

'You sure?'

'Yep. I've slept on a lot less comfortable in my time. And besides, we've got protection. Makes me feel all secure, knowing that there's two beefy blokes sitting outside to protect us. I told Frankie she should stay too, but you know her. Said we had to live our lives.'

'Listen Roxie,' said Margaret, suddenly serious. 'This thing could get nasty. Extremely nasty. What someone did to Joyce…' She didn't finish.

'I can cope,' said Roxie. 'You think opening a business on the Costa del Crime is a piece of cake? A woman on her own. I've had my share of hard visitors looking for a slice of the cake, and some of them wouldn't take no for an answer.' She wondered if this was the time to tell Margaret everything, but hesitated again.

Margaret shook her head. 'Dolly, what have you been up to? I never realised,' she said.

'You weren't supposed to. None of you. But for a while I was sleeping with a shotgun under the bed.' And a Derringer in the cash drawer, she thought.

'Blimey!'

'Blimey's right. Now listen. It's getting late, we should both get to bed. This film is crap, and I need some sleep if we're going to take on the world – and shopping on Oxford street.'

38

Margaret was up before anyone else and woke Roxie with a cup of tea. 'I'm going off to give my statement to Mahoney about finding Joyce,' she said, as her sister sat up in bed, honey-blonde hair sitting in a halo above her head. 'Then we'll go to London.'

'Fine. I'll get dressed. Thanks for the tea, sis,' said Roxie, in a voice fuzzy with sleep.

The two left the house before Sharon and the children came down, Margaret leaving a note on the kitchen table to tell them they'd be back in the afternoon. She drove down to the police station and left Roxie in the car in the visitor's parking area. 'I won't be long,' she said.

'Give him a kiss for me,' said Roxie, already fiddling with the tuner for the radio.

Margaret just sighed in exasperation.

She went to the front desk and asked for Mahoney, who came down a few minutes later and took her to an empty office. She recounted the story of finding Joyce's body and he transcribed it onto a computer, printed it out and passed it over so she could sign the bottom of the page. 'What now?' he asked.

'I'm off to London with Roxie to pick up a few things and have a scout round.'

'Remember – be careful.'

'I'll be okay, but thanks for your concern.'

'Let me know what you find if anything,' he said.

She nodded in reply and got up to leave, but before she left asked him, 'Anything yet on Joyce's murder?'

'Nothing,' he replied.

'You will let me know? A favour for a favour, remember?'

'I remember, and I will.'

'You've got my number. Just call me and I'll be there.'

'Thanks Mahoney – Mike,' she smiled at him and left the way she'd come in.

39

Roxie and Mags headed up the A3 through the late rush hour and managed to arrive in Battersea before eleven. Margaret parked up in a resident's bay and they went to her flat. 'Nice digs,' said Roxie when they got inside.

'It does for me. It's just a rental. Hard to get on the property ladder in London on a copper's wage.'

'A bit spartan though.'

'What do you mean? No fluffy cushion covers or stuffed animals on the bed?'

'Something like that. In fact there's nothing much at all really.'

'Send me a straw donkey in a sombrero when you get home then. It'll cheer the place up.'

'Don't get antsy. I only said,' said Roxie, giving her sister a hard look.

'Too much sometimes.'

'Calm down sis, I didn't know you were that sensitive.'

'So what's the plan?' asked Roxie, changing the subject.

'I'll get some clean things, and we take my guns and I'll go for a sniff round.'

'This Antarctic Holdings place?'

'Well, that's where we start.'

'You gonna go on your own?'

'In the first place. It's not for you this Dolly.'

'Will you be armed?' said Roxie, looking apprehensive.

'No. Not immediately. It's not a good idea until I've seen what kind of security they have. I'll leave the guns with you.'

'So, where are they now?'

'Come see.'

Margaret led the way to the gun safe on the wall, opened the door and stepped back.

'Empty,' said Roxie, disappointment in her voice.

'Don't you believe it,' said Margaret and manipulated a small lever that opened the false bottom, revealing her two illegal weapons and ammunition. 'Go ahead,' she said, with a smile.

Roxie hefted the Colt .45. 'Chase told me his granddaddy had one of these,' she said, wistfully. 'Antique.'

'They might be old, but clean, and untraceable.'

'I wasn't complaining,' said her sister, working the action with an oily click. It moved smoothly. 'Sweet. You look after them.'

'Never know when you'll need a gun,' said Margaret. 'You sure that one's not too big for you?'

The gun looked massive in Roxie's little hand, the dull grey metal bringing her hot pink nails into sharp relief. She shook her head. 'I like them big,' she said. 'The bigger the better. Guns and blokes.'

'Don't be disgusting,' said Margaret, but she laughed anyway, as she took the .38 revolver from its hiding place. 'I'll get a bag for this lot.'

Roxie began to take out the boxes of ammunition revealing a leather wallet at the bottom of the box. 'What's this?' she asked.

'My other identity,' said Margaret. 'A snide warrant card. That's how I intend to get inside Antarctic Holdings and find our Mr Haywood.'

'Blimey, you're showing our hand aren't you?'

'If I don't, the real police will catch up to us pretty damn quickly.'

'So what are you going to say?'

Margaret shrugged. 'I'll think of something. Come on, let me find some clothes, get these stashed away and let's go.'

'Got any more coke?' asked Roxie, a glint in her eye.

'You're a glutton aren't you?'

'Well, have you?'

'A bit.'

'Lay one out then. A livener for the day ahead and all that.'

Margaret went into the kitchen, took down a container marked 'mixed herbs,' opened it, and dug out a wrap. 'Not very original,' she said. 'But it does.'

She laid out two long lines on the kitchen top and the women snarfed up one each.

'So good,' said Roxie. 'Can we get some more?'

'Fancy a trip to my drug dealer, do you?' said Margaret.

'I love the low life.'

'OK. On the way back. It's a bit early for him, he

doesn't get to bed until 5am most nights.'

'Lovely,' said Roxie. 'Might as well finish this up then.'

'Sure.'

Margaret found a baseball cap in her wardrobe, plus a scarf to wind round her chin and a pair of sunglasses to hide her eyes. 'Look like me?' She asked her sister.

'No chance,' said Roxie.

'Perfect then. Let's go.'

40

—◦—

Once in the car, the guns and luggage stashed in the boot, Margaret headed across the river in the direction of Kensington.

'Do you think he'll fall for it? asked Roxie. The drugs had made her more alert but her heartbeat had slowed after the initial buzz. 'This Haywood bloke. You reckon just marching in and giving him the third degree will work?'

'Why not? I do a good impersonation of a copper you know. At least I should do.'

They found a parking meter near the office block and Margaret left Roxie in the driver's seat of the car. 'Don't know how long I'll be,' she said. 'You stay here. Keep the meter fed. Don't want the car towed away. It would be embarrassing trying to explain what's in the boot.'

'I'll be OK,' said her sister. 'I promise I won't move.'

Margaret climbed out of the driver's seat, pushed coins into the meter, and walked the short distance to the block. According to the register in the foyer, Antarctic Holdings was on the top three floors, nineteen to twenty-one. Margaret was impressed at the slick entrance to the imposing glass and steel building. She took the lift to the nineteenth, the floors above being blocked. Better security than Monty's, she thought.

When the lift doors opened she was in another foyer, faced by a reception desk manned by a pretty young black woman. She walked across and the woman smiled. 'Good morning,' she said through red-glossed lips. 'How can I be of help?'

'I'd like to see a Mr Haywood,' said Margaret.

'Do you have an appointment?'

'No.'

'Then I'm afraid that's impossible.' The smile had slipped slightly.

Margaret took out the fake warrant card and flashed it in front of the woman's face.

'Detective Constable Joan Hartley, Kensington station,' she said. 'Police business.'

The receptionist's smile had gone completely. 'I'll ring his secretary,' she said, picked up the phone and punched in three digits. She waited for a moment before speaking, 'Gina, there's a police woman here to see Mr Haywood.'

There was a pause. 'I see,' said the woman and replaced the receiver. 'I'm afraid Mr Haywood is out of the office today.'

Margaret didn't believe a word of it, but there was little she could do. 'Is there anyone else available?' she pressed. 'This is important. Very.'

'I could try Mr Sincere,' said the woman, obviously flustered.

'Sincere?' said Margaret.

'Saint Cyr,' the woman explained. 'Pronounced Sincere.' Margaret could tell by her tone she wasn't keen. 'Head of security.'

'He'll do,' said Margaret.

Once again the woman used the phone but this time she got a positive result. 'He'll be down in two minutes,' she said, her tone icy. 'Would you care to take a seat?'

41

Margaret elected to stand, and a few minutes later a tall, balding, slim man in a beige suit entered through a door on the left of the foyer. 'Detective,' he said. 'Peter St Cyr. How can I help you?' he said, his smile never reaching his eyes. He looked to be in his late forties.

'Can we talk privately?' said Margaret.

'Can I see some identification first,' said the man.

Margaret showed him the warrant which he examined closely, peering at the photograph for longer than seemed necessary. 'Constable Hartley,' he said, shaking her hand. 'Come up to my office.'

He led the way back through the door to another, smaller lift, went up one floor, turned left through more doors, along a wide corridor to an office at the end. It was large, well furnished with a breathtaking view over the park. There was a sofa and armchair by the window next to his desk and he motioned her to sit while he sat in the chair opposite. 'Very well,' he said. 'What can I do for you, Constable Hartley?'

'I came to see a Mr Haywood,' said Margaret. 'I believe he's the CEO here.'

'Correct. Concerning?'

'Concerning a Mr Monty Smith.'

She saw a flash in his eyes – it vanished almost immediately, but Margaret noticed.

'I don't think I'm acquainted with the gentleman,' he said.

'He was at a meeting with Mr Haywood at a hotel in Lovedean, near Southampton, three nights ago.'

'It's the first I've heard of it.'

'That may be so. On his way home he was involved in a car crash and died.'

'I'm very sorry. That's a tragedy.'

'Quite,' said Margaret, keeping her eyes fixed on his at all times. 'Then yesterday, we discovered his office had been broken into, and some time later, his employee – a Joyce Moody – was found dead. Murdered in her own home,' she said, her eyes boring into him, in her best interrogation mode.

'This is appalling. Where are we talking about?'

'Guildford.'

'Let me check,' he rose from his seat, went to his desk and started to type on his computer. 'Monty Smith, you say?'

'Yes. He was an accountant.'

'Ah. Yes. Here we are. Goodness. We have used his professional services regarding a promotion on the south coast. But it was last year. Nothing since.'

'So why was he at the meeting?'

'I don't know. Security is my forte. Perhaps another promotion? We do them from time to time,' said St Cyr, coming back to sit on the chair.

'Promotions for what?'

'We have many irons in many fires. That project last year was a new-build office development in Portsmouth.'

'But Mr Haywood would know, I assume,' said Margaret.

'I'm sure. Unfortunately…'

'Yes I know,' interrupted Margaret. 'He's "out of the office" today.'

'Precisely.'

'Then I'll make an appointment. I do need to speak to him as quickly as possible – as I'm sure you'll understand.'

'Please do. Is there anything else?' said St Cyr, making it clear that he wanted to be rid of her as quickly as possible.

'Not for now.'

'Then I'll show you out.' He wrote a number on a card. 'This is his PA's direct line. I'm sure she'll slot you in at a convenient time for you both.'

'Good. Thanks.'

He led the way back down to the reception and waited for the lift. 'Good day detective Hartley,' he said. 'Please be sure to send our condolences to his family.'

'I'll do that.' And when the lift arrived she entered, pressed ground, and was sure she saw another flash in his eyes as the door closed. Not a pleasant one.

42

⟫•❮

Margaret went back to the car where Roxie was waiting patiently. 'How did it go?' she asked.

'Crap,' said Margaret. 'Haywood was out so they said, and I saw their head of security. Peter *Sincere*,' she mocked.

'Sincere? What you on about? What was the place like?'

'Really swanky. Someone's doing well for himself. And it's spelled S-T-C-Y-R, just pronounced sincere.'

'What's he like?'

'More oil than my motor. Denied all knowledge at first, but it was plain to see that he knew something. Then, surprise, surprise, he found Monty in his records, said he'd done some work for them last year. But knew nothing about any meeting. Could be a future promotion, he said.'

'What?'

'Some bollocks about Monty doing a bit of work on a promotion for a new building in Portsmouth.'

'Why would he?'

'Precisely. It's too vague. Why would a firm in Kensington use a firm in Guildford? Monty was up to something – and he pissed somebody off. Pissed them off enough to make it worth killing two people for.'

'What now?'

'I dunno. I'll grill Mahoney when we get back.'

'He must really fancy you if he's given you inside information. What happens if they find out some fake copper looking like you has been sniffing about?'

'Then I'll lose my job good and proper. But I don't care. I was fond of Joyce. And Monty. Well, he *was* family – and Peter and Susan's dad.'

'My heart goes out to those little mites. I know how they feel.'

'Right, let's get back, stash the pistols and see what else rotten has happened.'

'Pessimist.'

'Just the way I feel right now.'

'Then we'd better get something to liven us up,' said Roxie. 'Is it still too early to go and see a man about a dog, if you know what I mean?'

43

———»•◦•«———

Margaret dug out her mobile, and speed dialled a number. After a moment, she said, 'is Boy there?'

A pause.

'Then you'd better wake him up then.'

Another pause.

'Just tell him it's an old friend from Denmark Hill.'

A longer pause, and Margaret said, 'lazy bastards.' Then, 'Boy. Sorry to disturb your well earned rest, but I need something.'

A pause.

'Now, say half an hour, depends on the traffic. See you then.'

She clicked off the phone and smiled at Roxie. 'No probs,' she said. 'When I say jump, that boy says "What roof?"'

They drove off, and Margaret headed south towards Loughborough Junction, one of the seediest parts of south London. She stopped outside an old LCC estate built just after World War Two, and not improved by the passage of time. 'You coming?' she said to Roxie. 'Meet the lovely Boy and his harem.'

'You'd better believe it,' said Roxie. 'But will your car be OK? You know with what's in the boot – and I don't like the look of those kids on bikes over there.'

'Good point,' said Margaret. 'There's a Tescos round the corner. I'll stick it in the car park. They've got CCTV, so the Porsche should be okay. Should be all right there for a bit. We won't be long.'

She did just that, taking a ticket from the barrier and stashing the car as close to the entrance as was possible. The car didn't stand out so much beside the other top end Chelsea tractors parked there. 'Gentrification,' she said to Roxie. 'Can't get away from it. Buy a great big house round Brixton for peanuts, but expect to be burgled once a month. The locals love it. Nice plasma screens and DVD recorders by the dozen. Straight onto eBay. Best fence in the world.'

'Cynical,' said Roxie.

'Comes with the job,' replied her sister.

They walked back to the estate, where children of all shapes, sizes and colours regarded them with hostile looks as they cut through, past garbage bins piled high with rubbish, over dog-shit encrusted pavements to the block where Boy lived. 'Nice,' said Roxie. 'And I thought Spain was bad. Shouldn't that lot be at school?'

'Just practising for a life of crime,' said Margaret.

They climbed graffiti-sprayed stairs to the top floor and along to the end flat where Margaret hammered on the door. It was opened by a young black girl in a low cut dress. 'Boy,' said Margaret.

The women stepped back and gestured with her head for them to enter.

They stepped into the hall which was hung with old velvet curtains, and squeezed past a brand-new black and silver mountain bike leaning against one wall. In the doorway in front of them appeared a young white man with long blonde dreadlocks that reached almost to his waist. He wore a T-shirt with the motto 'Don't Mess With The Boy' on the front, low slung blue jeans, more holes than material, and bare feet. He looked whacked out and bleary eyed. 'Bit early ain't it?' he said.

'The streets are aired,' said Margaret. 'And we've got places to be.'

'So who's this lovely lady?' asked Boy, looking at Roxie.

'Never you mind,' said Margaret. 'You got something for me?'

'Sure,' said Boy, producing a plastic baggie full of white powder from one pocket and giving it to Margaret. 'Only the best.'

'How much?' asked Margaret.

'I'll put it on your tab,' said Boy. 'I trust you.'

'I hope my tab's not written down anywhere,' said Margaret.

He tapped his forehead. 'No chance,' he said. 'It's all up here.'

'Nice bike,' said Roxie.

'Three grands' worth,' Boy said proudly.

'I wonder if there's a post code on it,' said Margaret. 'And I wonder if it's this one.'

'From what I hear these days that's none of your business,' said Boy with a smirk. 'Not doing much policing at the moment. At least that's what I hear.'

Margaret grabbed him by the throat and pushed him up against the wall. 'You hear too much,' she said. 'I can still get this place busted.'

'Leave him,' cried the black girl.

'And you,' said Margaret. 'Do you need to be nicked for soliciting.'

'It's no crime to talk to men,' said the black girl.

Just then a young white girl, who appeared to be no more than thirteen or fourteen, appeared at the doorway, carrying a can of Fosters.

'What's she doing here?' demanded Margaret.

'Picking up some stuff for her dad,' said Boy.

'How old are you?' Margaret asked the girl.

'Who's asking?'

'Police.' She gave Boy the evil eye, and he said nothing, just shuffled his feet on the filthy carpet.

'Old enough,' said the girl.

'Boy,' said Margaret. 'You want a visit?'

'No.'

'Then get her out of here.'

'Marsha, you'd better split,' said Boy. 'We'll catch up later.'

'But…' said the girl.

'No buts,' said Margaret. 'Hop it, and don't come back.'

The girl scowled, but did as she was told, and left.

Margaret pocketed the baggie, and said to Boy, 'if you're messing with her, I'll find out.'

'No messing,' protested Boy. 'Just a punter. Dad's a bit under the weather.'

'OK,' said Margaret. 'But be careful.'

'You too,' said Boy. Then, to the girl in the low-cut dress, 'come on, let's go back to bed.'

Roxie and Margaret went out the way they'd come in and headed back to the car park. 'Nice friends you've got,' said Roxie.

'Arseholes,' said Margaret. 'No friends of mine. But useful.'

'You were quite scary in there,' said Roxie.

'That was the idea.'

44

<hr>

Back in south Kensington, Peter St Cyr spoke to the receptionist as soon as Margaret had left. He went back to his office and used the phone, then went up to John Haywood's office, a scowl on his face. 'We've got trouble,' he said, when the door was closed firmly behind him.

'We always have when the police come calling,' said Haywood.

'That is the trouble. It wasn't police,' said St Cyr.

'What do you mean?'

'She told Sophie that she was from Kensington police station. I called them. They've never heard of a DC Hartley. Male or female.'

'Isn't it your job to know the local law?'

'I do. Well, the higher echelons anyway. Not every lowly DC. And her ID was authentic. At least it looked like it.'

'Maybe you'd better expand your horizons in future.'

'Sure. But right now I need to find out exactly what her game is.'

'You should never have accommodated her. Just fobbed her off like I did.'

'I didn't know what she wanted. Could have been anything. Tickets for a police social. We do try and keep in with the law. We bloody have to.'

'But she was fake.'

St Cyr nodded.

'Then how the devil did she get my name, and the company name? And what did she want to talk to me about?'

'How the devil should I know?' said St Cyr, sardonically.

'Don't try to be amusing Peter.'

'I'm not. She knew about Smith. And the meeting before he died.'

'Did she, by God. How come?' spluttered Haywood.

St Cyr shrugged. 'And she knew about Smith's death, and his bloody secretary too. I didn't give anything away of course, but she put me on the backfoot.'

'You're not paid your huge salary to be put on the backfoot Peter.'

'Fine. But then I'm not paid enough to be an accessory to murder. Two murders.'

'You've done worse where you've been.'

'This is England. That was some godforsaken part of bloody Africa. It's not the same.'

'Calm down. We didn't know it would come to this.' Haywood's brow was creased.

'I don't know how the hell we ever got involved with some provincial bloody amateur who I wouldn't let handle my cleaning lady's wages, let alone bloody millions.'

'Precisely because no one would suspect him of doing

what he was doing.'

'And he ripped us off.'

'Smarter than he looked.'

'Or we were dumber.'

'It happens. But that's only one of our pressing problems. This fake copper is the issue for now.'

'Sure.'

'You'd better find out who she is.'

St Cyr nodded. 'We've got her on CCTV.'

'Then get on with your job Peter.'

'I will.' And with that, he left.

When he was alone, Haywood picked up the phone. 'Gina,' he said, 'get me Trent up here. I've got a job for him.'

45

Trent was in Haywood's office almost before he put the phone down. 'You wanted me sir,' he said.

'Yes,' said Haywood, easing himself back in his leather executive's chair. 'There's something I need you to do.'

'Anything you say sir.' Trent was not a particularly big man. And this had fooled many an opponent to underestimate him. But he *was* hard and ruthless, and had killed before and was prepared to kill again for anyone who would pay him, and pay him well.

Haywood smiled. 'That's what I like to hear. We have more problems.' He explained about the fake police detective and her questions about Monty and his secretary.

Trent frowned. 'But surely that's Peter's project.'

'I think Peter's conscience may be getting to him.'

'Well, he's not as young as he used to be.'

'He seems to be rather squeamish about this job.'

'I've never known Peter to be that.'

'Times change. People change. Peter's on the hunt for our impostor. But you have other fish to fry.'

'So what do you need sir?'

Haywood explained what he wanted and mentioned a bonus that made Trent's head spin with thoughts of a new car and even a new flat. The fact that it enmeshed him in a conspiracy that could see him in jail for a very long time didn't even enter his head.

46

Margaret and Roxie stopped for a late lunch on the way back to Guildford, choosing a gastro pub off the A3 where they could keep an eye on the car from the window of the restaurant. 'What's the plan?' asked Roxie over the meal.

'No plan,' said Margaret. 'We'll have to busk it. Soon as we get back to the house I'll call Mahoney. See if he's got any news.'

'Would he tell you if he had?'

'I think so.'

'My, my, he is a naughty boy – or he just wants to get in your knickers.'

But when they arrived back at Sharon's, things had gone from bad to worse.

She and Frankie were waiting for them, huddled together, white faced on the sofa. There was no sign of the children.

'What's the matter?' asked Margaret.

'I had a phone call,' said Sharon, in a voice barely

above a whisper. 'A man. He wants money.'

'What?'

'He said that Monty had stolen money. Lots of money. And if I don't pay…'

'When?'

'Half an hour ago.'

'Why didn't you call me?'

'I didn't know what you were doing. I didn't think.'

'Well we're here now. Have you told anyone else? The coppers outside?' Margaret said anxiously.

'No. I wanted to see both of you first.'

'What else did this man say?'

'If I didn't pay he'd hurt the children. He knew all about us. Even knew their names,' Roxie gasped.

'Where are they?'

'Upstairs in Susan's room. I didn't want them to get scared,' said Frankie.

'Do you know anything about this money?' asked Margaret, softly.

'You know Monty never talked about his business. Well, only to say if it was a good year or a bad one.'

'And nothing about Antarctic Holdings or a bloke called Haywood?'

Sharon looked mystified. 'Who are they?'

'Someone I think Monty was working for. Someone dodgy.'

'Leave this to the police Mags, they know what they're doing,' interjected Frankie.

'We could all be dead by the time they figure it out,' Margaret retorted.

'What am I going to do?' wailed Sharon. 'I'm scared for the kids.'

'We'll have to get you out of here, somewhere safe. You, *and* the kids,' said Mags.

'Monty's mum's?'

'No. We don't want anyone else in harm's way. It'll have to be a safe house somewhere.'

'The man told me not to go to the police,' said Sharon worriedly.

'Course he did. But I am. I have to. I'm going upstairs to talk to that copper who came here. Roxie. You come as well. Bring the bags. If the phone goes again, come and get me immediately.'

The two women went to Margaret's room, leaving Frankie comforting a trembling Sharon. 'This is getting out of hand,' Mags said, her voice grim.

'Tell me about it,' said Roxie, unloading the bag of guns and bullets. 'Lock and load,' and she broke open a box of .45 ammunition, and started to fill one of the spare clips of the big Colt. 'Whoever's foolish enough to mess with the Doyles needs to back off. But this will help them get that message.'

'Little sis, you bring a tear to my eye. Mum would have been so proud.'

47

Margaret took out her mobile and dialled in the number Mahoney had given her. He answered at once. 'There's been a development,' she said.

'What?'

'Someone's threatened Sharon. They're demanding money. Money she hasn't got.'

'Threatened her how?'

'Someone called when I was out today.'

'I'll be right there.'

Mahoney was as good as his word, and they opened the door to him ten minutes later. He and Margaret took Sharon into the living room. Sharon was still shaking and deathly white. 'Have you used the phone since he called?' he asked, to which Sharon shook her head.

Mahoney called to the police station on his mobile to see if they could track the call. 'What did this man say?' he asked.

'He said Monty had stolen money. He wanted it back. I told him I didn't know anything about any money, and then he threatened my children.'

'No. Just said that he'd hurt them – and me. He told me not to go to the police. They won't hurt them, will they,' she asked Mahoney, beseechingly.

'No, don't worry, you did the right thing. We're going to look after you and the kids, but we need to get you somewhere safe.'

'I don't want to leave here,' Sharon wailed. 'There's the funeral. Funerals, now Joyce is dead.'

'We'll handle all that,' said Margaret.

'And school…?'

'I think school is out for the moment,' said Mahoney. 'I've already got a place in mind. After what's happened, and now this…' He didn't finish.

'I suppose you're right,' said Sharon. 'I just don't like leaving. What will Peter and Susan think?'

'It's the best for all of you,' said Margaret, holding her sister's hand. 'Believe me.'

'What sort of place?' asked Sharon.

'A house. A cottage really. Out in the country. But not too far. It'll be an adventure for your children,' said Mahoney.

'I suppose,' Sharon said, bleakly.

'Why don't you go and pack,' suggested Margaret. 'Tell the kids it's a holiday.'

Sharon nodded. 'I suppose so. If you think I should Mags.'

'I do love, honestly,' said Mags, cajoling. 'We just need to get you somewhere safe. You and the kids. This is the best place for you, under the circumstances.'

'Then I will. Thank you Sergeant.'

'I'm just sorry it's come to this,' said Mahoney.

'Not as sorry as I am.' And with that, Sharon got up and left the room.

48

———⟫•⟪———

Mahoney and Margaret were still sitting in the living room when his mobile rang. 'Anything?' he said into it, obviously recognising the caller. 'Bugger,' he said after a moment. 'Thanks anyway.'

He shut it off, then shook his head at Margaret. 'Call box,' he said. 'London. Trafalgar Square, if that means anything.'

'We might have guessed.'

'And what have you been up to?'

'Went back home, got some stuff. Clothes, you know.'

'Anything else?'

Margaret shook her head. She thought it best not to mention her visit to Antarctic Holdings, and certainly not the fact that she was now armed. 'What about you? Have you heard anything more about the case?' she asked.

'Like I said yesterday, I'm on the sidelines. But at least I could fix up a place for your sister and her children to stay.'

'I'm grateful. This is getting out of hand. Anything from Monty's office or Joyce's place?'

'Nothing. Not that I'm supposed to know anything. But I keep my ear to the ground. By the way, about the funerals. They might have to wait a while. We don't want to release the bodies right away. Is that going to cause problems?'

'There's nothing that can be done if it does,' Mags was resigned.

'Yes. I'm sorry about that.'

'Not your fault Mahoney. Anything more on this Haywood character?'

'He's a bit dodgy to say the least. South African but he left when apartheid fell apart. Bit of a colonial our Mr Haywood. Liked the *status quo* if you know what I mean. And not the band.'

'Liked the natives in their place you mean?'

'Exactly. Had fingers in diamond mines and all sorts. Apparently didn't treat the workers too well. A lot of people died on his watch. Some from accidents that could have been prevented. Haywood wasn't big on health and safety, to say the least. And then there were others.'

'Others?'

'Yeah. The bosses don't like the workers trying to smuggle out the gems. Rough justice if they're discovered. A bit of torture. A bit of ultra-violence. A bit of bodies being found buried in shallow graves with their stomachs cut open in case they swallowed the merchandise.'

'Lovely. So what was the connection to Monty?'

'Your brother-in-law did some work for him apparently. Small beer though, according to our enquiries.'

Exactly what that smooth bugger St Cyr told me, thought Margaret. 'Do you believe that?' she asked Mahoney.

'Until I learn something different, I do. Now, I'll stick around and take your family to our safe house. Is that OK?'

'Of course. You're doing us a big favour.'

'My pleasure,' he said with an involuntary grin, which he quickly stifled.

49

Eventually Sharon, the children, Frankie and Roxie came into the room. 'I've packed for a week,' said Sharon. 'I just pray that's enough.'

'We're going on our holidays,' said Susan to Mags, brightly. 'To the country. I hope there's ponies.'

'There might be,' said Margaret, feeling a slight pang of sadness at the sight of her innocent niece so happy. 'This is Mahoney. He's your driver.'

Mahoney looked quizzical, but said nothing.

'He's a nice man,' said Margaret. 'He might even buy you lollipops.'

'I don't want a lollipop,' said Peter. 'I want my dad.'

Sharon hugged him. 'I'm sorry love,' she said, 'I wish he was here too. You have to be a big strong boy for him now.'

'Well, I want a lollipop,' said Susan.

'Come on then,' said Mahoney. 'My car's outside. Maybe we can stop on the way. Get those lollipops, or something.'

'Hooray,' said Susan and clapped her hands. 'And Auntie Mags, be sure to look after Thomas.'

'I will,' said Margaret, hugging Sharon tightly and kissing the kids goodbye. On the way Mahoney said to her, 'Look, I'll keep in close contact, but to be on the safe side I'm not going to tell you the address where we're going.'

'Nor would I under the circumstances,' said Margaret.

'But of course you can keep in touch on her mobile.'

Margaret nodded.

'And we're going to keep a presence outside, but not a permanent one now the children are gone. So be careful.'

'We will,' said Margaret. 'Don't worry about us.'

Roxie, Frankie and Margaret waved off the family then went back inside and closed the door.

'I bet he'll keep in close contact,' said Roxie. 'As close as he can to you Mags.'

'Yeah, yeah, yeah.'

'I don't know what to do with myself, now they're gone,' said Frankie.

'How about a drink,' said Margaret.

'Tea or coffee?'

'I was thinking of something stronger.'

'Good idea,' said Frankie. 'I'll go and get some ice out of the fridge, and we can get off our heads. I think we deserve it.'

'Me too,' said Margaret.

'What now?' said Roxie, when Frankie had gone into the kitchen.

'Now they've started to threaten the kids we go on the offensive. They don't know who they're dealing with here.'

'Fine,' said Roxie. 'Offensive it is.'

Mags continued. 'We need someone on the inside on the outside.'

'Bleeding hell, Mags, this isn't Dempsey and Makepeace. I'm a beautician, tell it to me in terms I'll understand.'

'That Saint Cyr bloke looked like a ladies man,' said Margaret. 'And you're a lady.'

'What are you suggesting?' said Roxie, quizzically.

'You've heard of a honey trap, right? Happens all the time in cases. You'd be surprised how many pimps and dealers are caught this way.'

'So you've done it?'

'No. Not really my thing. Don't look the part.'

'And I do?'

'In a word, yes.'

'Terrific. How old is he?'

'Forties, I think.'

'Well, I always did attract older men.'

'It's your scintillating personality sis. Or your big tits.'

'Thanks Mags! My lils have always worked for me, that's true,' Roxie said good naturedly.

'I reckon you'd be perfect at it, always were a little drama queen. So are you up for it?'

'But I dunno sis, how do we even get close to him?'

'I'm going to go up to London for a few days. I'll have a scout around and suss him out,' said Margaret, mentally working out her plan.

'But he's seen you. Won't he recognise you?'

'Me? The mistress of disguise? Don't forget I spent a long time undercover as a cop. I think I can blend in with the background, and he'll never even know I'm there.'

'Should I come with you?' said Roxie.

'No. I'm keeping you under wraps for now. You stay down here, keep Frankie company – she looks a bit lost. If I need you I'll call. You've got Sharon's car if you need transport?'

'OK, but I don't like it.'

'It's not a case of liking it or not love. If we do this, we do it right. Go all the way and bugger the consequences. This is deadly serious.'

'I know all about serious.'

'Course you do. So what's it to be. In or out?' Mags looked directly at her sister.

'In of course.'

'I knew you would.'

'But I still don't like it.'

Roxie felt the cold grip of fear on her heart once again. She just hoped that this time, her intuition was wrong.

50

Margaret told Frankie she had to return to London, but
kept her real plans secret, telling her sister that she had
business to attend to at the flat in Battersea. Frankie
seemed listless and unhappy, but cheered up a little
when Margaret told her Roxie would be staying in
Guildford. 'I'm glad that Dolly is staying here. The
house is quiet without Sharon and the kids,' said
Frankie.

'I'm going to go now,' Mags said. 'Beat the rush hour.'

Mags left most of the clothes that she'd brought with
her and took only the necessities – a wrap of cocaine and
the Colt revolver. She got into her car and sped up to
Battersea where she quickly went into her bedroom and
donned a blonde wig, a cheap trench coat and her Gucci
dark glasses, a different pair from the ones she had worn
when she had met Saint Cyr earlier. Then she drove to
Kensington, parked close to the Antarctic Holdings
building and waited. It was well past seven by then, and
she hoped she hadn't missed Saint Cyr, but if she had

she'd have to come back the next night. She figured the head of security wouldn't be a clock watcher and she was right. She pulled the car across the street, not too close to the front doors but where she could keep an eye on the entrance to the building's car park. In the glove compartment of the Porsche she had a small, powerful pair of binoculars which she used to scan the cars leaving the building, cursing the fact that she was doing a solo surveillance. She sat there for half an hour, and then saw Saint Cyr leave the building on foot and head off in the direction of Kensington High Street. By then it had started to rain and he was dressed in a Burberry macintosh and carried a brightly coloured golf umbrella. Margaret got out of the car and followed him at a discreet pace – the brightly coloured umbrella made him easy to spot. She kept her distance until he came to a smart looking bar and restaurant about halfway down the street and entered. It was easy to spot him in the brightly-lit room and she watched through the plate glass window as he went up to the counter, sat on a stool, and was immediately served by the barman. It looked like he was a regular, as the two engaged in conversation. Margaret pulled up the collar of her coat, walked into the bar and sat at a small table on the far side of the room.

A young waitress approached and she ordered coffee and an overpriced sandwich from the menu, keeping half an eye on Saint Cyr, who was now talking animatedly to another customer as if they were old friends. Margaret kept her eyes fixed on him as she ate her sandwich and she saw Saint Cyr being greeted by other patrons, but never joining any of them, instead remaining alone at the bar. He had two drinks and left. Margaret dropped enough money on the table to cover her bill and a tip, and followed him out of the bar, as Saint Cyr returned to his office building, but this time went down into the car park. Margaret ran back to her car, which had been ticketed, but luckily not clamped, and waited. A few minutes later a dark blue Lexus pulled up the ramp from the parking area; Saint Cyr in the driver's seat. He turned left and Margaret followed him through the heavy traffic. It was only a short drive to Fulham, where Saint Cyr parked on a residents' bay, and walked towards a grand looking town house where he let himself in. The house was in darkness until lights came on in the hall and the downstairs front window – which told Margaret that he lived alone.

Perfect, she thought.

51

Margaret figured she'd seen all she was going to see that night and, as it was coming on for ten o'clock, she headed back to Battersea. On the way, her mobile rang. Like most other people on the road, she ignored the law and answered it, hands on. It was Mahoney. 'Where are you?' he asked.

'You don't even want to know,' she said.

'Yes I don't doubt that… I'm just calling to tell you your family are settled at the cottage. It's not too bad as safe houses go, but not as comfortable as home. There's a WPC keeping an eye.'

'That's good,' said Mags, relieved.

'But when I got back to the station there'd been a funny phone call.'

'Funny, how?'

'It was from Kensington nick. They got a call from head of security at Antarctic Holdings this morning. Seems like *someone* was impersonating a copper and asking questions. Young female DC, name of Hartley.

Course, there's no such person *in* the Met. From the description though it sounds like someone I know,' he said pointedly. 'Anyway, the bloke turns all cagey when he finds out this DC Hartley doesn't exist. They asked to view the tapes, but he says the CCTV on their floors was off-line, and plays hard to get when our boy asks what sort of questions she was asking. But I'd put money on the fact it was about a certain Monty Smith. What do you reckon?'

'No comment.'

'As I thought. Anyway, the DS who picked up Haywood's call was intrigued. Wandered round and got a look at the cameras on the ground floor, and there she was. Baseball cap, shades, leather jacket with the collar up, scarf round the face. Right sus I'd say. The security at the front door gave her a tug, but she flashed her warrant and they let her pass. He went back to the station and had a trawl through the computer. Seen the red flag of course, then that we'd been checking and gave my super a bell to put him in the picture.'

'Good for him,' said Margaret, coolly.

'Any ideas about who this fake copper could be?'

'There's some wicked people out there.'

'You can say that again. If, and I only say if, it was you – you could've put yourself in harm's way. Look what happened later at your sister's place.'

'Just as well it wasn't me then,' she said shortly.

'So you say. When are you coming back down to Guildford?'

'Can't say. A couple of days at least. Got some things to take care of down here first.'

'OK. Well take it easy.'

'Always.'

'Goodnight then. See you soon I hope.'

'You really sound like you mean it Mahoney,' said Mags, teasingly.

'I do.'

'Goodnight Mahoney, sleep tight.' She closed her phone with a snap.

She got back to Battersea, parked up, went indoors, poured a glass of wine, trying to watch TV, but found she couldn't concentrate, so she finished her drink and went to bed.

The alcohol failed to make her sleep, and she tossed and turned as she went through the events of the day. Why Monty? He was just a provincial accountant. Why would Haywood, with all the trappings of an international company, employ such a man? It didn't make sense. But he had, and Monty had paid the price of dipping his toes into shark-infested water. He had been an innocent abroad. Or had he? It was a dilemma that she was no closer to solving as a distant clock struck three.

52

—————⋟⊙⋞—————

The next day passed slowly as she pottered around her flat and waited for the evening to arrive. She phoned Roxie and Frankie, they had nothing to report but she was relieved that there had been no more threatening calls. Around five she put on her blonde wig and completed her disguise with the same dark glasses she had worn the previous evening. She left the Porsche at the flat and took a cab to Kensington, and went straight to the bar to see if Saint Cyr was the regular she imagined him to be. She sat at the same table and ordered coffee and a sandwich just like the night before. She had the same waitress too, who remembered her. 'Hello again,' she said. 'Have you moved in round here?'

'No,' replied Margaret, smiling. 'Just visiting. Sightseeing, you know. Catching up on old friends.'

'Not from London?'

'Originally. Moved on.'

'You staying long?' asked the young blonde waitress, a chatty Australian.

'No. Just a few days.'

'Well, enjoy.'

'Thanks.'

At seven Peter Saint Cyr came in, alone, made a beeline for the same seat at the bar that he'd sat at last night and was greeted by the barman who poured him a drink without asking.

Excellent, thought Margaret. A creature of habit. Easy to track.

Saint Cyr seemed to know most of the customers, but never engaged in conversation with them too long. He smiled at the women, and flirted with the waitress who cleared Margaret's dishes when she had finished her meal. 'I'll have a glass of dry white,' she said to her, keeping St Cyr in the corner of her eye.

'Sure,' nodded the waitress as she rushed to the bar to get her drink.

When she returned with the drink Mags said to her, 'he seems to be enjoying himself', nodding in Saint Cyr's direction.

'Who, Peter? Yes, he's a regular. In every night when he's in town.'

'Seems like a nice bloke.'

'If you like that sort of thing. He's a bit handy, if you know what I mean. But he brings in a lot of trade at lunchtime. Business lunches, so we have to be nice,' said the waitress, indiscreetly.

'Oh, one of those,' said Margaret knowingly, filing away the info for future reference.

'Yeah,' replied the waitress. 'Enjoy your drink.'

This should be easy, Margaret said to herself as the waitress left.

53

Margaret sipped her drink and watched as Saint Cyr played the most popular man in the bar. He drank two drinks, then left, wishing everyone a good night. Margaret didn't follow, just finished her wine, left the waitress a decent tip and went home in a taxi.

Like the previous evening she poured herself another glass, switched on the TV, but didn't follow the plot of the *CSI Miami* that was showing. Around midnight she went to bed, only to be woken by the phone as the digital display on her bedside clock showed three am. Feeling a deadly sense of *deja vu*, Margaret hooked the receiver off its stand. 'Yes,' she said.

'It's me, Roxie. You've got to come back.'

'Why?'

'It's Sharon. She's taken an overdose.'

'Oh God, no,' cried Margaret.

'And Peter found her, when she didn't come in and say goodnight. Frankie's with them now at this safe house place.'

'Christ, I can't believe she would do that. Not Sharon. She loved those kids. Did she leave a note?'

'No.'

'Stupid cow.'

'No sis, think about it. She's been through it lately. Monty, Joyce, then those threats. She just couldn't cope. You know Sharon was always the soft one.'

'But Peter and Susan? Why put them through this? After everything that's happened to them recently?'

'You know Monty was her life, Mags. She must've been desperate,' Roxie persisted.

'I know how she feels. Was anyone there with them?'

'The copper acting as liaison or whatever you call it. She got an ambulance.'

'Thank Christ for that. At least the kids weren't on their own. What's the prognosis? Are you at the hospital?'

'She's still unconscious, but alive.'

'I'll be with you as soon as I can. See you later,' she replied and put down the phone. She got out of bed, and got dressed. Christ, she thought again, unable to take it all in. These bastards have got something to answer for. And they will, if I have to go to prison for the rest of my life.

54

Margaret sped through the empty streets of south London down to the motorway and on to the hospital in Guildford. She was getting tired of the drive and felt nauseous with the panic gripping her empty stomach.

She found Roxie pacing up and down outside the entrance of the hospital. 'What's the story, Dolly?' Mags demanded.

'Glad you're here. Its not looking good, but there's no change sis. Come on, let's go up and see her.'

They went upstairs to the side ward where Sharon was in the only bed; tubes and wires poking out of her mouth and body. The machines next to the bed were bleeping quietly and Margaret took her hand. 'Why Sharon?' she said. 'Why do this to all of us?'

'She did it to herself,' said Roxie.

'No. To us and the kids. Where are they by the way?'

'Still at the cottage with Frankie. She thought that one of us should be there when they woke up.'

'That's the best plan. Do they know?'

'Not really.'

'Sister or no sister of ours, this was a bastard thing to do.'

'Don't be so hard, Mags.'

'We've got to be hard. The kids need her more than ever and this is so selfish. Where's her doctor?'

'That one there,' said Roxie, pointing towards a youngish, prematurely balding man in green scrubs heading their way. 'Doctor Ramsey.'

Margaret buttonholed him in the corridor. 'Doctor Ramsey,' she said. 'It's about Sharon Smith. I'm her sister Margaret. Is she going to be all right?'

'It's a waiting game at the moment,' said the doctor. 'She took a massive overdose. We pumped her stomach of course and we're just monitoring her for now. It was lucky the ambulance got there so quickly. I'm sorry I can't be more specific.' He went to Sharon's bedside and checked the monitors. 'She's breathing and her lungs are clear. She's sleeping quietly. That's all I can tell you. We're close by, and doing everything we can.'

'Can we stay?' asked Margaret.

'If you wish, but it could be a long night.'

'We'll manage,' said Roxie, eyes fixed on her sister in the bed.

55

It was almost dawn by then and the next few hours did indeed pass slowly for Roxie and Mags sitting by Sharon's bed. Although they both prayed for some sign of recovery, Sharon hardly stirred as the nurses and her doctor came and went. Margaret used the time to explain to Roxie about her observation of Peter Saint Cyr and her plan for him and his associates.

'Saint Cyr is the key to this. We grab him and find out everything he knows,' said Margaret. 'And then, if it's true they were behind Monty's and Joyce's death, we'll go straight in and sort out this Haywood character.'

'And if it isn't what we think?'

'Believe me, we're right,' said Margaret. 'Copper's instinct.'

'OK. I trust you sis. Then what?'

'Then we will do what needs to be done. These people have fucked with us once too often. I want a full confession.'

'This is dangerous you know. We could both end

up arrested, or worse.'

'Sure. Listen Dolly, if you want out just say so. No hard feelings.'

'And if I did?'

'Then I'll carry on in my own sweet way and come up with another plan. Roxie, I've had enough of being pushed around. That's what happened to me in the force. I turned into the bad guy through no fault of my own – then all this started. To be honest with you Roxie, I was half convinced to turn in my papers anyway. It's all changed being a copper. Health and safety and hours of paperwork, and what thanks do you get? Fuck all. Why should I waste any more of my life on the force when it doesn't give a fuck about me? I care about my family and they're my priority now. I don't care what happens to me, I just wanna get the fuckers that harmed my family. So what's it to be?'

Roxie looked at the prone body of her sister in the bed next to them, so pale and quiet, and looked at her sister with a determined glint in her eyes. 'Mags, I think it's time I told you a thing or two about myself.'

56

'Like what?' asked Margaret, perplexed.

'I haven't been telling you the truth since I got back. Well, you know some of it, but I've done some bad things.'

'What have you been up to Dolly? I know you had a little dabble with drugs but you didn't do anything too bad, did you?'

'That's not the half of it. Remember I told you about the bloke in America? Chase?'

'Sure. Your cowboy lover.'

'That's him. Well, he died,' said Roxie, her voice cracking.

'I'm sorry love. How did it happen?'

'Shot dead whilst taking part in an armed robbery.'

'Bloody hell. When?'

'When I was with him.'

'With him? You mean like his girlfriend?'

'No – well, yes. But *literally* with him. I was driving.'

'In an armed robbery?' exclaimed Mags. 'But I

thought you went back to the ship.'

'I was crazy about him. I jumped ship in New Orleans and stayed with him for two months. He told me he wasn't the rich kid I'd taken him for and actually made his money knocking over banks. I told him about Mum, and about our background and he said that we made a good couple. We ran out of dough after a while and needed to get some more, quickly. His old partner was in jail. He saw the way I drive, and how I liked shooting, and we did a couple of jobs. The second one went wrong. He was shot by the cops and bled to death in the back of the car. I dumped the body, and got away. He told me to. I think he really loved me too.' By this time tears were running down Roxie's face, unchecked.

'And I thought I was in trouble,' said Margaret, hugging Roxie tight.

'That's not all,' said Roxie.

'There's more? God you have been busy little sis...'

'That's not the half of it. I went to Spain, opened the salon. I had a bit of money, borrowed the rest from a 'friend,' if you know what I mean. Cash was easy come, easy go on the Costa in those days. I hooked up with another bloke. Tony. I knew him from my days in the club scene in London. Bit of a dangerous bloke – finger in a lot of pies.'

'And?'

'He was a bastard. A bit handy if you know what I mean.'

'I know exactly what you mean,' said Mags.

'We split up and the business went down the pan. I told you about sleeping with a shotgun under the bed? Well, I had another gun too. Before I came back to the

UK, Tony came looking for some money he said I owed him. He conveniently forgot that most of it went on bubbles and Charlie for the two of us, living the high life. He threatened me with a knife. Said he was going to rape and then kill me if I didn't pay up, so I shot the fucker.'

'Classic self-defence Dolly. I would have done the same in your situation.'

'Yeah, but I've had trouble with the police in Spain too. There were some dodgy cheques I cashed for dodgy people so I tried to stay out of their way. Couldn't exactly go crying to them now.'

'But even so…'

'I took him out the morning I got the call about Monty. I couldn't hang about. I knew I'd end up in some stinking jail so I dumped the gun and headed here.'

'So you're wanted?'

'Expect so. The temperature was pushing thirty degrees. Someone was sure to find the body before long.'

'Jesus, Roxie.'

'So you see, I don't give a toss either. I'm in this with you Mags – whatever happens. Unless of course you want to turn me in.'

'What do you reckon, Dolly?'

The two sisters hugged again as the machines beside Sharon's bed bleeped on.

57

When Margaret and Roxie woke up the next morning they were still in the hard plastic chairs next to Sharon's bed. Hearing the sound of breakfasts being served in the other wards, they both realised they were starving and asked the Irish nurse on duty if they could get some breakfast themselves, or at least some coffee. She pointed them in the direction of the canteen on the ground floor, and promised to find them if Sharon's circumstances changed, although she didn't seem too optimistic. 'When this sort of thing happens, I've seen people sleep for days. It's the body's way of healing itself,' she said. 'But don't worry, I won't be far, and I'll keep a close eye on your sister,' she said in a kindly tone.

The two sisters took the lift downstairs, and both bought cooked breakfasts from the canteen. 'I feel rotten, stuffing myself when Sharon's upstairs like that,' said Roxie.

'We need to eat,' said Margaret. 'We need to be strong. Starving ourselves won't help.'

Roxie nodded agreement, and they found an empty table and sat down.

They'd finished their meals quickly and Margaret said, 'I need a cigarette.'

'So do I.'

'You don't even smoke sis!'

'I'm thinking about taking it up. I'm as nervous as hell about all of this. What if I can't get this St Cyr bloke to believe me?'

'What you? The scourge of clubland. I thought pulling blokes was one of your great talents and you're a good little actress. Remember all those times that you convinced Dad you were tucked up in bed when you were actually out drinking cider in the park with the bad lads from school?'

'It is true, I can usually get my way with blokes. But not in order to kidnap them. At least – not often.'

'Come on,' said Margaret. 'Let's go outside for a minute. Get some fresh air.'

'And some smoke.'

'That too.'

They went out of the front door and both lit up. It was a beautiful morning, but the fine weather did little to cheer them up.

As they finished their cigarettes, Margaret recognised Mahoney's car as it sped into the car park in front of them. He jumped out and ran towards them, unshaven, his hair sticking up in all directions.

'Isn't he sweet,' said Roxie. 'All warm from his bed. Look at what you're missing,' she said, grinning.

'Shut up.'

Mahoney slid to a halt in front of them. 'Jesus, I just

heard,' he said. 'What happened?'

'She OD'd on sleepers,' said Margaret. 'She's sleeping in the ward upstairs.'

'Do you think she did it on purpose?' said Mahoney.

'Who knows. She didn't leave a note.'

'Christ. Could this get much worse?'

Neither of the women replied.

'I'm so sorry,' said Mahoney.

'Always sorry,' said Margaret. 'Come on, let's get upstairs.'

58

The three of them got in the lift and went back upstairs to the side ward, where things had got worse. Much worse. Sharon's bed was empty, and the machines were dead. 'No,' said Roxie, her face crumpling.

As they went outside into the corridor, the Irish nurse they'd seen earlier ran up, Doctor Ramsey just behind her. 'We tried to find you,' the nurse said. 'We had you paged.'

'We were outside,' said Margaret. 'Just for a minute.'

'I'm so sorry,' said the doctor. 'She crashed. We did what we could…'

'You mean…' said Margaret, her words trailing off as she realised what had happened.

'Your sister died a few minutes ago of a coronary. There was nothing we could do,' said the doctor in a hushed tone.

Roxie let out an anguished wail and Margaret had to grab her to stop her from collapsing.

'We tried to resuscitate,' said the doctor. 'Her body couldn't take it.'

'But so quickly?' said Margaret, disbelievingly. 'We were just here?'

The doctor made a gesture of defeat. 'It just happened. Nurse was there at her bedside. She called a code immediately. There was nothing more we could have done.'

Margaret and Roxie just stood there in the hallway, their arms around each other, the sound of Roxie's sobs filling the air. Mahoney stood behind them, hopping from foot to foot in frustration.

'Would you like to see her?' asked the doctor. 'Before we take her downstairs.'

'Yes,' said Margaret holding onto her sister tightly.

They followed the doctor into a sterile room down the corridor where Sharon's body lay on a gurney. Mahoney stayed outside, his face grey.

Both the women kissed their sister's face which was already beginning to cool. 'How are we going to tell Frankie and the kids? They've just lost their dad – now they're orphans?' asked Roxie.

'We'll manage,' said Margaret, her face set with determination. 'Between us, we'll cope.'

59

They went back outside to where Mahoney was waiting. 'Where's this cottage?' asked Margaret. 'We need to get there now.'

'Not far,' replied Mahoney. 'Maybe twenty minutes. But it's a bit hard to find. I'll drive you if you like.'

'No, I've got my car,' said Margaret. 'You lead the way, we'll follow.'

'OK. For what's it worth, I am really sorry to hear about Sharon. This case has claimed too many lives already.'

They found the doctor and told him they were leaving to break the news to the rest of the family. 'I understand,' he said. 'And once again you have our profound sympathy.'

'Thank you,' said Margaret. Roxie could only nod, her face swollen from crying.

The three went down to the car park where Roxie joined Margaret in the Porsche. Mahoney pulled out in front of them and headed away from Guildford with

Margaret following close behind. Roxie dabbed at her eyes. 'This is going to be hard,' she said.

'I know,' replied Margaret. 'Those poor kids.'

'What will happen to them?'

'I suppose Frankie will look after them. There's no way our niece and nephew are going into care. But it'll be hard on her.'

'She's a natural mother, she'll be okay. I just hope we're around to lend a hand,' said Roxie, turning to look at Mags.

'It's not too late to just forget all about Haywood,' said Margaret.

'You're kidding. Sharon's dead because of him. Even more reason to see that fucker gets what he deserves.'

'If we're right,' said Mags, a faint tone of uncertainty entering her voice.

'I thought you were sure. Copper's instinct.'

'I don't know what I am right now.'

'Listen. This is no time for second thoughts. You're the one wanted a hundred percent. Right?'

'Right,' said Mags.

'We know they're at it. And it could only have been them that killed Monty and Joyce.'

'But we don't have any hard evidence,' Mags hated to voice her fears but she needed reassurance.

'So what? We know. We don't need hard evidence. Only to get one of them to crack. What would Mum have done? Waited for hard evidence? I don't think so. She worked on instinct. You must've done too to get as far as you did in your job.'

'Yeah,' said Mags. 'You're right. And you're more like Mum than any of us. Sorry. Bottle went a bit there.'

'I understand sis. So when do we do it?'

'Tomorrow.'

'OK, tomorrow it is,' said Roxie looking through the windscreen at the back of Mahoney's car. 'He really likes you, you know. So do something about it.'

'No time.'

'There's one more night – tonight. If the last few days have taught us anything, it's that you've got to grab life in both hands. Just go for it Mags. What have you got to lose?'

60

Mahoney led them off the A3 close to Guildford, then onto a number of minor roads. They weaved through a couple of small villages, then onto a bumpy track through a wood just big enough for one car, that opened up onto a turnaround with a small cottage at one end. They recognised Frankie's car but not the other plain, dark saloon parked outside.

They got out of the Porsche and the air was silent except for the rustling of the leaves of the trees. 'Idyllic,' said Roxie. 'Ain't that the word?'

'Not when we break the news,' said Margaret. 'I'm not looking forward to this.'

'Me neither,' said Roxie, her eyes welling up again.

They walked together to Mahoney's car and he wound down the window. 'Want me to come in?' he asked Margaret.

'No. This is our job.'

'I'll be going then.'

'No. I need to speak to you. Don't go. Please.'

'Sure,' said Mahoney. 'I'll park up over there.'

'I may be a while inside.'

'Of course. There's no hurry. Take as much time as you need.'

As Margaret stepped away from the car the door to the cottage opened and Frankie walked down the short path to the gate. Margaret took Roxie's arm and they joined her. Frankie was white faced and her eyes were swollen. 'Don't tell me,' she said. 'I can see by the look on your faces.'

'It's bad news,' said Margaret, softly.

'When isn't it, lately?'

'There's no way to make this easy,' said Margaret. 'Sharon died an hour ago.'

Frankie grabbed hold of the gate and she closed her eyes. 'What have we done to deserve this?' she said with a voice they hardly recognised. 'What? Why is this happening to us?'

'We've done nothing,' said Roxie. 'This is no time for blame. Those two inside need us now more than ever.'

'How are we going to tell them?' said Frankie, her voice thick with tears.

'The three of us will,' said Margaret. 'Together.'

61

Peter and Susan were cuddled up to the policewoman on the sofa in the cottage's tiny living room when the three sisters got inside. 'Can we have a moment alone?' asked Margaret.

The police woman nodded and left the room. Margaret, Roxie and Frankie went to the children at the sofa, Roxie and Frankie sitting either side of the children, their arms around them. Margaret said, 'Peter, Susan, I'm afraid I've got bad news.'

'Where's mummy?' asked Susan.

'Mummy's in heaven with daddy,' said Roxie. 'I'm so sorry, my darlings.'

The two children looked at each other with expressions of disbelief, their faces quickly contorting with sobs. 'No,' said Peter. 'She said she'd look after us.'

'I'm going to look after you now,' said Frankie, and she gathered them into her arms. 'Me, and Auntie Roxie and Auntie Mags. Aren't we?' she said looking at the other two. 'We'll always be here for you.'

Both nodded, and Frankie pulled Susan onto her knee as Margaret took Peter in her arms. All five sat together in silence, broken only by the children's long anguished sobs. They stayed together until both Peter and Susan fell asleep from exhaustion. 'I'm going to take them home,' said Frankie. 'This place gives me the creeps.'

'Are you sure?' said Margaret.

'Why not? Monty, Joyce and Sharon are all gone now. What more can these people – whoever they are – do to us now? They would never hurt the children. You know Monty, he was a good man. He would never have got mixed up in anything too bad.'

Margaret looked at Roxie. 'We don't know what he was involved in. But three people are dead,' she said. 'I think you'd be safer here for the time being.'

'Okay. Whatever you think is best,' said Frankie, her voice flat.

'I'll stay too,' said Roxie. 'Margaret needs to see that copper Mahoney tonight to catch up with what's going on.'

'Fine,' said Frankie.

'He's waiting for me outside,' said Margaret. 'I'd better go and see him.'

She carefully extracted herself from her sleeping nephew and went outside where Mahoney was talking to the female officer.

She moved away from the car when she saw Margaret. 'I'm sorry about your sister,' she said. 'She was a nice woman.'

'Thanks,' said Margaret. 'And thanks for being here and calling the ambulance.'

'Just doing my job. They were very quick, if that's any consolation.'

'Some.' Margaret nodded at Mahoney's car. 'I just need to speak to him for a minute.'

'Of course. I'll go and make some tea. That's all you can do at a time like this. How are Peter and Susan holding up?'

'As to be expected,' said Margaret. 'Orphaned in less than a week. They're exhausted.'

When the woman left, Margaret joined Mahoney in his car. 'I owe you dinner,' she said.

'Don't worry about that.'

'I'm not worrying, but I do owe you dinner,' she repeated.

'Fine. We'll make a date,' Mahoney said.

'Tonight.'

'Are you sure?'

'It has to be tonight,' said Margaret, her tone a little more forceful.

'Well, if you insist. I'd like that. Shall we go to the Chinese place again?'

'How about a take-out at your place?'

Mahoney's brow furrowed. 'Is that a good idea?' he asked. 'Today of all days... Wouldn't you rather be with your family?'

'We need to talk, and it would be best out of earshot,' she said, decidedly.

'Give me your address.'

Mahoney wrote it on a piece of paper from his note book. 'It's just outside the...'

'I'll find it,' said Margaret, cutting him off mid-flow. 'Seven do you?'

'Of course.'

'And thanks for waiting for me.'

'No problem.'

'And for Christ's sake have a shave,' said Margaret, grinning slightly.

'Whatever you say,' Mahoney replied, returning her half smile.

Without another word Margaret opened the passenger door, got out of the car and went back into the cottage.

62

Margaret and her sisters spent another bleak day consoling each other and Sharon's children. The mood in the cottage was grim. Peter and Susan didn't understand what was happening. How could they? One day they were a happy family doing the sort of things that happy families did. The next they were orphans. The three women were as bereft as the children, but tried not to show it with little success, although they were careful not to cry in front of them. Around four Margaret left and went back to Sharon's empty house. She could hardly bear to be there surrounded by family pictures from happier times but she needed some time alone, plus time to get ready to see Mahoney. She felt guilty about leaving the family, but there was little that she could do for them at the moment. She told Roxie she'd collect her the next morning. 'Have fun,' she said as Margaret left, her face puffy from crying but her eyes twinkling slightly as she spoke.

'I don't know if I should go,' said Mags, suddenly unsure.

'Course you should. Remember what I said – life's too short. I'll hold the fort here.'

Margaret considered what she was wearing when she got to her room. Jumper and trousers. Not exactly an outfit to drive men wild, she thought. But she had nothing better and could hardly touch anything of Sharon's under the circumstances. Then she saw the bag of clothes that Roxie had brought with her. What the hell, she thought, let's see what little sister has stashed away.

She opened the bag and found a selection of clothes. She passed on the thongs. So last year Roxie, she thought, but found some lacy shorts-style knickers with a matching bra, a tight pencil skirt and a silk blouse. She tried them on and they fitted perfectly. Still the same size, sis, she thought. Not bad for five years older than you.

She left her legs bare and slipped into her high heeled ankle boots, laid on some slap and felt ready for anything. Mahoney, you don't know what you're in for, she thought as she brushed her hair. She left the house about six-thirty and sped off in her Porsche for Mahoney's house.

63

Margaret found Mahoney's address with little trouble. It was a modern block on the outskirts of Guildford near the cathedral and university. She parked in a visitor's bay, checked her make-up in the rear view mirror and went to the front entrance. She rang the bell for his flat and waited, feeling nervous at the thought of going on a date after so long – if you could call it a date, when really she just wanted some good sex. After a few seconds of indecision, when she actually thought she might turn and flee, she heard his voice on the speaker. 'Push the door, and come up,' he said, as a buzzer sounded.

Here goes nothing she thought, as she did what he said, entering the foyer and calling the lift. Mahoney's flat was on the top floor, and he was standing at his open door when the lift opened. She was pleased to note that he *had* shaved and combed his hair, and he was dressed in blue jeans and a pale blue polo shirt, his aftershave smelling clean and fresh.

'You're punctual,' he said, smiling. 'Come on in.'

She followed him down a short hall into a sizable living room, one wall of which was glass, with a view of the massive tower of the cathedral. The room was sparely furnished with a sofa, leather swivel armchair, a coffee table, a big screen plasma TV and top of the range stereo system, and a couple of bookshelves crammed with paperbacks.

'Bachelor pad,' she said. 'This is very nice. Must be good money in being a copper these days,' she said, her tone teasing.

'Just renting. Wherever I lay my hat, as they say.'

'Good plan in our game.'

'Drink? I have beer, wine, red or white. Scotch, gin, you name it.'

'Wine would be good. White.'

'Sit a minute. It's in the fridge.'

Mahoney went back into the hall and into the kitchen, where Mags heard him open and close the fridge door. He returned with an open bottle of wine and two glasses. By then Margaret was sitting on the sofa, her skirt up around her thighs, and she knew Mahoney noticed. He put the bottle and glasses on the coffee table, filled both and handed her one glass. He joined her on the sofa and they clinked their glasses together. 'Cheers,' he said.

'Cheers,' she replied.

'So what do you want to eat?' he asked. 'Pizza, Chinese, Indian, Thai. The whole culinary world is just down the road, only a phone call away.

Margaret crossed her legs and her skirt rose even higher. 'Can we eat later?' she asked. 'Frankly right now, after the day I've had, I'd just like to go to bed.'

64

'You don't beat around the bush do you?' said Mahoney, surprised at her words.

'After what I've seen in the past few weeks, especially today, I don't have time to waste. Life can be very short, and who knows where we'll be tomorrow. I've lost my bloody sister, I'm feeling like shit. I feel guilty about what happened to her, and guilty about just being here when I should really be with my family.'

'You have no reason to be guilty. None of this is your fault. So why *are* you here?'

'To forget for a few hours.'

'And I'm just handy, I suppose?'

'Look Mahoney, this is what it is. If you want me to go, I will.'

'I never said that.'

'I'm not just using you Mahoney. I need a friend. They've been in short supply for long time.'

'Just a friend?'

'You know what I mean. You want to don't you?'

'You know I've wanted to, since the first time I saw you,' Mahoney said softly.

'But you made a good job of pretending not to like me.'

'It was hard, but I was here for the job.'

'And it's hard now isn't it?' She looked at his crotch inside his tight jeans.

Mahoney actually blushed, then laughed. 'I've never met anyone like you before, Ms Doyle,' he said. 'Got me'.

'At least for tonight,' she said, standing up and taking his hand. 'Bring the wine,' she said, smiling at him seductively.

They went out of the room and Mahoney led her to the bedroom. It was barely furnished but the double bed, wardrobe and dresser looked expensive. 'Nice bed,' said Margaret. 'Nice and big. I see you're prepared for visitors.'

'Came with the place,' said Mahoney, putting the bottle and his glass on top of the dresser. 'And I've always flown solo before now.'

'It'll make a nice change for you then,' said Margaret as she dragged him over to the bed and peeled back the duvet. 'Now undress me for fuck's sake and let's get this show on the road.'

She turned and asked him to unzip her skirt, which he did. She let it drop to the floor and stepped out of it facing away from him. When she turned back he'd taken off his shirt. 'Nice bod,' she said. 'I had a feeling it would be. You must lay off the pies in the canteen.'

'Always liked to keep in shape,' he replied. 'You never know what the day will bring.'

'No you don't,' said Margaret, and she went into his arms and they kissed. Gently at first then harder, until her head swum, and it wasn't the drop of wine she'd drunk that caused it. She wanted to forget about everything for a few hours – and Mahoney helped her do that.

65

When they were both satisfied, they lay back on the damp sheets. 'That was good,' said Mahoney.

Margaret said nothing.

'What do you think?' he asked.

'Thai,' replied Margaret. 'Light, but spicy.'

'No, I mean…'

'I know what you mean Mahoney,' she interrupted.

'Mike. Now we're friends.'

'I like Mahoney better though.'

'Fair enough Mags. They call you Mags don't they? Your family. I will too if you don't mind.'

'If you want,' she said shortly.

'You're always the hard woman. But you were soft when we made love.'

'Did you say 'love', Mahoney? That wasn't love – that was sex, pure and simple.'

'Next time it might be.'

'If there is a next time after tonight. You see Mahoney, we're in a bubble. And that bubble could burst,' she said in a hushed voice that betrayed her true feelings.

He held her tightly and she didn't push him away. 'I know who did it,' she said, muffled into his chest.

'Did what?'

'Killed Monty and Joyce, and made Sharon kill herself.'

Mahoney held her at arm's length and looked deeply into her eyes. 'How do you know?'

'It's bloody obvious.'

'But can you prove it?'

'No. I just know.'

'So what are you going to do about it Mags?' he asked.

'I'm going to get revenge,' she replied. For the first time she allowed her emotions to take over, and she cried real tears until the damp sheets were even damper.

66

'You shouldn't say something like that to me,' said Mahoney, looking worried.

'Why not? Because you're a copper?'

'I care about your safety, you know. But yes, because I'm a copper too – as are you, don't forget.'

'In a compromising position though. What would your DI say if he could see us now?'

'He'd probably say lucky old me,' he said, smiling.

Margaret laughed and dried her tears on the sheet. 'Sorry,' she said. 'Mascara. Might not come out.'

'I don't mind. It'll remind me of you.'

'You're a real romantic Mahoney, you know that. I bet you even send Valentine cards.'

'It has been known.'

'I'll have to give you my address.'

'It could be Holloway, if you meant what you said,' Mahoney turned serious for a moment.

'Forget it. I got emotional. I must've caught it from you.'

'What now then?'

'Like I said. Thai.'

'Are you going to stay?'

'Why? You want me to fuck and run?'

'Just the opposite.'

'Then I'll stay,' she said, looking at him directly.

'Good. I'll find the menu from the restaurant.'

Margaret got out of bed, grabbed her knickers, and Mahoney showed her the bathroom. On the way she picked up her phone, locked the door and called Roxie. 'Had a good shag?' her sister asked when she answered.

'None of your business, little sis. We had a nice time, that's all you need to know.'

'Lucky girl,' Roxie laughed. 'He's a doll.'

'Listen,' said Margaret. 'No more waiting around. We're on for tomorrow. Right?'

'Right,' said Roxie, sounding hesitant.

'No time for second thoughts love, remember? Just think of mum. She would've done anything for her family, and so must we. Even if we end up in jail.'

'Of course. You don't think that will happen do you, Mags?'

'Not if I've got anything to do with it. Trust me. How's everyone else holding up?'

'How do you think? Not well.'

'It'll soon be over,' said Mags, determinedly.

'One way or another.'

'Right. I'll pick you up in the morning from the cottage. We need a throwaway phone so I can listen in to what's going on. We'll pick one up on the way into town. You sure you're up for this? I need you on-side Roxie. Remember, this is the only way that we can make sure the people responsible for Sharon's death get what they deserve.'

'I know Mags. I want that too.'

'OK then, I'll see you first thing.'

Margaret ended the call and washed her face. There was a towelling robe hanging on the back of the door and she slipped into it. It smelled of Mahoney, and she liked that.

67

———◆———

They ate in front of the TV with the sound turned down and the lights low as the sun set over the town. It was peaceful, and Margaret relished it, figuring it would be the last peace she'd know for a long time. Mahoney had dressed again, but Margaret preferred to wear his dressing gown. She knew it was stupid, but for once she didn't care.

After they'd eaten they began to fool around again, and eventually ended up back in bed. The sex was less desperate that time and lasted for hours. Almost like making love, thought Margaret, but dismissed the thought. Afterwards they lay together in each others' arms and went to sleep.

Margaret woke as dawn broke, and disengaged herself from Mahoney's embrace. He stayed asleep, and she thought of waking him for another go round, but knew it would only make it harder to leave, so she took her clothes into the bathroom, and quietly got dressed.

He was still sound asleep when she looked into the bedroom. Sorry Mahoney, she thought. But this is the best way, as she gathered her things and slipped out into the bright morning.

She drove back to Sharon's, showered quickly and changed into trousers, sweater and her trusty leather jacket. She got back in her car and went out to the cottage where Roxie was waiting by the gate. How is everyone?' Mags asked her little sister.

'All fast asleep. Do you want to come in and say good-bye?' asked Roxie.

'No,' said Margaret. 'We'll call them later.'

On the drive Roxie tried to tease Margaret about Mahoney, but her mood was grim and she didn't respond. Eventually she gave up.

They were back in Battersea early, and went over the plan again before Margaret went down to the high street and bought a prepaid mobile phone.

'I want some gear,' said Roxie when she got back.

'You sure.'

'Absolutely. I need something to keep sharp,' she answered.

'OK, I'll call Boy.'

She speed-dialled his number, and he answered promptly. 'It's me. Not too early?' she said.

'No. Been for a bike ride already.'

'Really? Never had you down for the sporty type.'

'You never know how things can change,' said Boy, cryptically.

'Sure. You sorted?'

'When haven't I been?' snorted Boy.

'See you in a bit then.'

She closed her phone. 'He sounds weird, probably trying to be a funny bastard,' she said. 'Come on, let's go.'

68

This time Roxie drove to Loughborough Junction, and once again they left the car in the supermarket car park.

They walked to the estate, past the usual crowd of kids, and knocked on Boy's front door. It was opened by the young black girl again, wearing a dressing gown, but with one eye swollen almost shut. 'What happened to you?' asked Margaret as she and Roxie went inside.

She didn't answer, just looked terrified as she slammed the door shut behind them. 'Sorry,' she said, her voice wavering.

'What?' said Margaret, as two men came into the hall, one from the living room and one from the kitchen. Both were thickset hard case types, both wore black bomber jackets and jeans and heavy lace up boots – and both were carrying baseball bats. 'Now, who do we have here?' said one of the men.

'What's going on?' demanded Margaret. 'Where's Boy?'

'Here he is,' said the other man, and pulled Boy out of

the living room. He was white faced and shaking, and he was bleeding from a badly cut lip. 'Sorry,' he said, wiping away some of the blood with the sleeve of his shirt. 'I couldn't warn you. I tried.'

'All that bike riding bullshit,' said Margaret. 'I might've guessed.'

'But you didn't,' said the man holding Boy, a horrid smile on his face. 'Your hard luck.'

'Hard luck for you,' said Margaret. 'We're police.'

'Bollocks,' said the first man. 'You're punters. Police don't phone and make an appointment.'

'Police,' repeated Margaret.

'Cagney and fucking Lacey,' said the first man. 'Better call for back-up then. Ain't that what you do on TV?'

Margaret said nothing.

'Cat got your tongue?' said the second man, letting go of Boy. 'Where's your radio? Stupid cow. Now he owes us, and I bet you're holding. So let's have your bag.'

He made a move towards Margaret, and Roxie spoke up sharply. 'Leave her.'

'It speaks,' said the first man. 'Bit tasty too. We were going to have fun with the spade, but we prefer white meat.'

'Fuck you,' said Roxie, pulling the big Colt automatic from under her sweatshirt, and pointing it at his head. The pistol still looked massive in her tiny hand, but she held it steady. 'It's old, but it's reliable,' she said, 'and it's full of hollow point bullets. If I shoot you in the face from this range it'll blow your head into the middle of next week.'

The black girl put her face in her hands and slumped back against the wall, crying silently.

'Now drop the bats,' ordered Roxie. 'And down on your knees. That's what they do on TV ain't it?'

'You wouldn't dare,' said the first man, but the blood was gone from his face.

Roxie cocked the pistol with a click that was loud in the silence of the flat. 'Try me,' she said calmly. 'I've done it before, and I'll do it again if I have to. Take my word for it. I might look like a pretty face but I will fuck you up with no hesitation.'

The bats hit the carpet as both men went down onto their knees.

'Why'd you bring that?' asked Margaret.

'Didn't like the vibes last time,' said Roxie. Then to Boy. 'No offence.'

'No offence taken,' said Boy. 'Christ I wish I had a sister like you.'

Roxie grinned, then ordered both men into the living room at gunpoint and made them sit on the sofa, hands under their backsides. 'So what do we do with them now?' she said.

'You owe them money?' Margaret asked Boy.

He nodded.

'Can't pay?'

He held both hands out palms upwards. 'Cash flow,' he said.

'Seems to me you've become too fond of your own product.'

'You know what it's like,' said Boy, sheepishly.

'OK,' said Margaret. 'You two. Wallets.'

They both pulled wallets from the pockets of their jackets. Margaret looked inside both for ID, then satisfied, she dropped both into her bag. 'I'm keeping these,' she said. 'Now, then boys. Trousers off.'

'Do what?' said the first man.

'You heard. Trousers off. One at a time. Roxie,' she said, turning to her. 'Seems like these boys can't hear properly.'

Roxie grinned and steadied her gun. 'Come on,' she said. 'Do what the lady tells you. Slowly.'

The first man stood awkwardly and lowered his jeans, exposing yellowing Y-fronts. 'Right off,' said Margaret.

He tugged his trousers off and dropped them on the floor.

'Sit down again', said Margaret. 'And you should get your mum to do your laundry.'

He did as he was told. 'Now you,' she said to the other man.

He obeyed. This time it was Union Jack boxers 'Patriotic,' said Margaret. 'The queen must be so proud of people like you. Right, off you go.'

'The car keys,' said the first man, a look of panic in his face. 'In my pocket.'

'Forget it,' said Margaret. 'There's a bus stop round the corner. Hope you've got change.'

'Have a heart,' said the second man.

'You beat up this young girl and you're asking me to have a heart,' said Margaret. 'You're lucky we don't give you a taste of your own medicine.'

The two men went to the door. 'We'll be back,' they said.

'Don't,' said Margaret. 'We know who you are, and we are police.'

The two men left, and Margaret watched them run out of the estate chased by the catcalls of the gang of kids.

'You'd better make plans for a holiday,' she said to Boy. 'A long one. I think we've pissed them off.'

'It was time for a move anyway,' he replied. 'What do you reckon Glo?' he said to the black girl.

'Hackney,' she said. 'I've got people there.'

'Sounds OK,' said Boy. 'It was getting old around here anyway.' Then to Margaret. 'I owe you one.'

'It's her you should thank,' she said, nodding at Roxie. 'She brought the gun.'

'Course,' said Boy. 'Thanks love. I owe you more than one. You da 'bidness,' he said in his fake whiteboy patois.

'A pleasure,' said Roxie. 'Brightened up a dull day.'

'So can I get you something?'

'That's what we're here for.'

'They never got the stash. You got here just in time.'

'Well come on then,' said Margaret. 'Get a move on, before those boys find some clothes.'

Boy went into another room and came out with a big bag of powder. 'Here you go,' he said. 'On the house, and your tab's clear.'

'Cheers, glad to hear it,' said Margaret.

'Right,' said Boy. 'Come on Glo. We'd better make a move sharpish.'

'Won't take a minute,' she said. Then to the sisters. 'You saved us. I'll never forget you. Those bastards meant what they said. They were gonna… They were gonna rape me. You should have heard what they were saying before you got here. Thank you,' she said, her voice full of gratitude.

'Just keep safe,' said Roxie.

'Keep in touch,' said Margaret to Boy. 'You've got my mobile.'

'Soon as we're sorted I'll give you a bell,' said Boy. 'I'd give you a kiss, but...' he pointed to his lip that was still bleeding, and shook them both by the hand. 'I mean it. You saved our skins. We won't forget.'

'See you then,' said Margaret, and she and Roxie left the flat. They didn't see either of the men on the way back to the car.

Once inside, she said. 'You done good there Rox. Would you have used it?'

'You better believe it,' said Roxie.

'Christ. Look at us, the lipstick killers. We're our mother's daughters, no doubt.'

69

After a few samples of Boy's thank-you gift, the two sisters left in Margaret's car for Kensington at six pm. Roxie had two phones. Her own, and the prepaid that Margaret had bought earlier, now fully-charged, and connected to Margaret's mobile line. Roxie was dressed to impress. Short skirt, killer heels and a jacket that emphasised her ample chest. The live phone went in the top pocket of the jacket, and the .38 revolver in her bag – just in case. They sat opposite the bar, and right on time Peter Saint Cyr arrived, dressed in a Burberry macintosh and a trilby hat. 'That's the fella,' said Margaret.

'Too smooth for my taste,' said Roxie.

'Don't worry. I reckon you're just up his street. Now go, girl, and remember you can do this.'

She left the car, crossed the street, went into the bar and sat at a stool in front of the counter, two seats down from where Saint Cyr was sitting. He noticed her immediately, as did every other man in the place. She looked at her watch with a frown and ordered a white wine spritzer from the barman. He produced it with a flourish and a smile which she didn't return, just looked at her watch again and tapped her foot impatiently on the floor.

Saint Cyr looked at her reflection in the mirror behind the bar and took a sip of his beer. Margaret had been right. Roxie was just his type, especially looking the way she did that evening.

Fifteen minutes passed and Roxie had hardly touched her drink, just kept checking the time before she took her own mobile out of her handbag and pretended to make a call. To Saint Cyr it simply looked like no one answered, and she pulled a face before switching the instrument off. That was when he made his move, standing and walking down towards her. 'Excuse me,' he said.

She turned and gave him a dirty look. 'What?' she said.

'Are you OK?'

'Why shouldn't I be?' Roxie snapped at him.

'Sorry. But I couldn't help noticing. You look like something's wrong.'

'If it's any of your business, which it isn't, I'm supposed to be meeting someone and they haven't turned up.'

'Then he's got very bad taste. He should be ashamed,' said St Cyr, smoothly.

'It's not a he, it's as she, as a matter of fact, and she's always doing this. Her phone's switched off and not even a bloody text.'

'Sorry again. But don't waste the evening. Can I get you another drink?'

'I haven't finished this one yet, and I should be going.'

'Don't go. This is a decent place, and it livens up later. Have you been before?'

'No.'

'Thought not. I'm a bit of a regular after work – and I'd have noticed you no doubt. Why don't you stay a while? Just a friendly drink. Anyway, your friend might have been delayed. She could still turn up.'

'Suppose so,' said Roxie, pretending to give it some thought.

'May I join you then.'

'If you want.'

Saint Cyr fetched his drink and took the stool next to Roxie. 'My names Peter, by the way.'

For the first time Roxie smiled. 'Peter. I'm Tessa. My friends call me Tess.'

'Pleased to meet you Tess,' he said, and they shook hands. While Peter busied himself ordering the drinks, Roxie took the chance to check that the phone in her top pocket was still running – that Mags could hear every word of their conversation.

70

<hr/>

After that, the evening went just as Margaret had forecast. After a shaky start, Tess and Peter began an animated conversation, and she seemed to warm to him more and more. It seemed that Peter was a big man in finance and security and Tess owned several beauty salons. 'You're too young, surely?' said Peter.

'Thank you, but I decided early on that I was going to be my own boss.'

'Very wise.' 'No boyfriend?' Saint Cyr had noticed that there were no rings on her left hand.

''Fraid not. No man can keep up with me. That's why it was a girl's night out tonight – or supposed to be. Makes a change from sitting in front of the box though. How about you?'

'No. No boyfriend,' said Saint Cyr with a laugh.

'You know what I mean.'

'They work me too hard at the office. That's why I end up here most nights, keeping the barman company.'

'Well cheers,' said Roxie, touching her glass to his.

'Looks like it didn't work out too bad for either of us,' she flirted.

An hour or two passed companionably as they sipped their drinks and chatted about inconsequentials – the weather, the US elections and the best restaurants in the West End, and Roxie said all the right things to make Saint Cyr sure he was onto a result.

'Listen,' said Roxie, checking her watch and seeing that it was close to ten pm, 'I really have to go.'

'Really?'

'Yes. I've got an early start tomorrow.'

'Where do you live?'

'Battersea,' she replied. 'You?'

'Fulham. Are you driving?'

'I don't drink and drive. I got a cab. You?'

'Yes. Company car parked at the office. That's why I stick to just a couple.'

Roxie smiled.

'Let me give you a lift,' he said.

'To Battersea?' said Roxie. 'That's right out of your way.'

'Nonsense. It's just a hop over the river.'

'You really don't have to leave on my account.'

He smiled at her charmingly. 'With you gone the evening would only go downhill.'

'Flatterer. But I like it,' she teased.

Saint Cyr smiled again, settled the bill for their drinks and they left together. They walked back to his building and Roxie waited on the pavement whilst he went into the parking garage. A few minutes later the Lexus appeared, and she got in. 'Nice car,' she said. 'You really must be important.'

'Oh, you know,' he replied with a modest grin.

Arsehole, she thought, but kept her painted smile in place.

He steered the car in the direction of the river, and once over Wandsworth Bridge Roxie gave directions to Margaret's street.

He parked the Lexus a few doors down from the house where Margaret lived, and turned towards Roxie. 'This has been a wonderful evening,' he said. 'Maybe we could do it again.'

'I don't see why not. But remember, no man can keep up with me,' she replied.

'Who knows, you might have just met one,' he said, and he kissed her on the mouth.

She responded back, even though she was repulsed by him, and said. 'You might be right Peter. How about coffee?'

'I thought you had an early start?'

'Forgive me, I don't usually act like this. Too many drinks perhaps,' said Roxie, turning coquettish. She had an idea that this attitude would make him putty in her hands.

'Or the company,' said Peter, a little too cocksure.

They both got out of the car, and walked the short distance to the flat, arms entwined. Roxie let them in with Margaret's keys. 'Upstairs,' she said as they entered the communal hallway.

She went first, and could feel his eyes on her backside, which she gave an extra swing as she climbed the stairs. She opened the front door to the flat itself and stepped back. 'Straight through,' she said and allowed Saint Cyr to lead the way. 'I always leave the lights on, hate coming back to a dark place alone,' she said.

'But you're not alone tonight,' he said, leering over her figure as they walked down the short hall. He walked through the open door of the living room where Margaret was sitting in the armchair facing the door – Colt .45 in one hand, her mobile in the other. 'Hello Peter,' she said. 'Welcome to our world.'

71

'You?' he said, recognising Margaret from her visit to the office. 'What the hell?'

Roxie shoved him roughly from behind and he stumbled into the middle of the room 'What's going on?' he demanded, a look of utter disbelief on his face

'Sit down *Sincere*,' said Margaret, and gestured with the gun to the sofa.

'I don't...'

'Just sit,' said Roxie who had pulled the smaller gun from her bag.

Saint Cyr did as he was told, a look of complete disbelief on his face. 'Is this a joke?' he asked.

'No joke,' said Margaret. 'Deadly serious, as you'll find out before long.'

'Did you hear it all?' asked Roxie.

'Every word. You're a smooth operator Peter, I'll give you that.'

'God, I actually kissed the old fucker,' said Roxie. 'Made me sick.'

'But he fell for it. You were very convincing.'

From his seat Saint Cyr looked from one woman to the other. 'What the hell is going on?' he asked. 'I don't understand.'

'Monty Smith,' said Margaret. 'Remember?'

Saint Cyr's face changed, and he began to rise.

'Don't,' said Margaret. 'These aren't toy guns, and we'll use them.'

'What would the neighbours say?' he said, challenging her.

Margaret pulled her police issue asp from the side of the chair, pressed the button that extended it with a snap, and smacked Saint Cyr hard on the knee. 'More than one way to skin a cat,' she said.

He cried out in pain, but sat back.

'That's better,' said Margaret, standing, the asp swinging in front of his face. 'Now – Monty Smith. Or do I have to prove I don't give a shit for you *or* the neighbours?'

72

━━━►•◄━━━

'I don't know what you're talking about,' said St Cyr, his eyes wild.

'Peter,' said Margaret. 'This is not going to work unless you tell us the truth. We're Monty's sisters-in-law. I'm a copper. We know that you're an errand boy for John Haywood. Monty's dead, so is his secretary, and my sister killed herself a few days ago. All because someone at your office threatened her and her children. Now don't fuck us about. Tell us the whole sorry story or *you'll* be bloody sorry.'

Saint Cyr looked at Roxie. 'Bitch,' he said, looking at her with hate.

Margaret swung the asp again and landed a blow on his upper arm. He squealed in pain. 'And less of that sort of talk. Roxie, keep him covered.' She put the gun and the asp down. 'Put your hands in front of you,' she ordered Saint Cyr.

He did as he was told, and Margaret cuffed his wrists. 'Right,' she said. 'Looks like we're in for a long night.'

She sat, and picked up the pistol again. 'Come on now, Peter,' she said. 'Spill the beans.'

'You're police?' he said. 'I don't believe you.'

'Where do you think I got the asp and the cuffs?' she asked. 'Army surplus?'

'And what's she?' He nodded in the direction of Roxie. 'Tess, or Roxie, or whatever her bloody name is.'

'What I said,' said Roxie. 'Beauty consultant. Well, ex-beauty consultant to be exact.'

'Who carries a gun?'

'Some of the ladies can get vicious,' said Roxie. 'But this isn't getting us anywhere.'

'So how long do you intend to keep me here?'

'As long as necessary,' Roxie said, shortly.

'I'll be missed.'

'Not tonight. You live alone, remember?' said Margaret.

'So what makes you think I know more about this Smith person than I told you on our last meeting?'

'You made a mistake,' said Roxie, shortly. 'You used your mobile to call the man who called my sister, and threatened her.'

'No I didn't,' he said. 'It wasn't me, it was...' he stopped.

'Gotcha,' said Margaret.

73

———✦———

'Listen,' said Saint Cyr, his voice beginning to whine as he finally realised the seriousness of his situation. 'I didn't want any part of it.'

'Threatening innocent women? Women with young children?'

'Exactly.'

'And what about killing Monty and his secretary?'

'That wasn't supposed to happen. Not killing him. It was meant as a frightener. The brakes were supposed to fail immediately. Not somewhere down the road at speed.'

'And Joyce Smart? Sliced like a Christmas turkey – are you saying that wasn't supposed to happen? I found her you know.'

'Not me again.'

'Then who?' Margaret picked up her gun and screwed the barrel into Saint Cyr's cheek. 'I'll kill you,' she said, her voice as cold as ice. 'I swear. Tell me the truth or I'll do it.'

'It was Trent. A young buck in the organisation, looking for points from Haywood. I'm head of security – killing women isn't in my job description.'

'But why Monty at all? What did he do?'

'He stole money. Lots of money.' Saint Cyr almost seemed relieved to start talking.

'What kind of money?'

'Dirty money of course.'

'From?'

'VAT fraud. Gold and diamonds from South Africa. Import, export, but cut out the revenue. Simple. But how do you know about any of that?'

'I'm a bloody copper,' said Margaret. 'It's my job to know things like that.'

'But not the copper you pretended to be.'

'I had my reasons.'

'So why Monty?' pressed Roxie.

'I met him at a school reunion. He was younger than me of course. We got talking, and when I told him who I worked for he asked if there was any work for him. Old school, you know what that means. I introduced him to Haywood, and it turned out he was an accounting genius. Christ knows what he was doing in Guildford doing the accounts for the local shopkeepers. We gave him more and more responsibility for the VAT. But then he got greedy and started ripping us off. We didn't mind a little. Comes with the territory. But he obviously didn't know who he was dealing with, because he just didn't stop.'

'So you killed him.'

'I told you, it wasn't supposed to happen. Then Trent's thugs got over eager and killed his secretary.'

'And threatened my sister.'

'Another stupid mistake. We should have just forgotten about the money, Christ. We thought it was all over when Smith's wife went off the deep end. We were prepared to cut our losses.'

This time Margaret hit him with the barrel of the Colt. 'Our sister, remember? Our dead sister.'

Saint Cyr was almost in tears by then. The urbane, cocky man of the world was gone, leaving a scared child in his place. 'So what do you want?'

'You, Haywood, and whoever else was involved.'

'Are you going to call the police? I mean, you'll be in trouble yourselves after what you've done to me. Kidnap, assault, false imprisonment.'

'You've been watching *The Bill* again Peter', said Margaret. 'Trouble is, I'm already up to my neck in trouble.'

'Me too,' said Roxie. 'Besides, I haven't had so much fun in years. You can't imagine how boring it is doing another Paris Hilton cut and colour.'

'Christ,' Saint Cyr said again, but under his breath this time.

'So we're all going to have a quiet night in,' said Margaret. 'And tomorrow we're going into work with you and we're all going to sort this out – one way or another.'

74

Margaret and Roxie kept Saint Cyr cuffed on the couch all night, just allowing him one toilet break and he complained bitterly at Roxie staying with him in the bathroom. 'You wanted to show it to me last night badly enough,' she said. 'Just do what you have to do, and shut up.'

The next morning Margaret drove the Lexus up to Kensington with Saint Cyr on the front passenger side with his hands free, Roxie behind him, with the big Colt .45 jammed into the back of his seat. 'I'll blow your spine through the windscreen if you get any ideas,' she said when they got moving. 'I promise you I will.'

'I believe you,' he said. 'But you don't have access passes to get inside.'

'Busk it,' said Margaret. 'You're the big security boss. Surely you give out the passes?'

'I'll do my best, I run a tight ship here,' he started, but stopped quickly when Mags glared at him.

'You'd better,' said Roxie. 'Or you're going to make

one hell of a mess on your nice leather upholstery.'

They got to the building about nine-thirty and Margaret swapped places with Saint Cyr in the street opposite, and he drove into the entrance to the underground car park. Roxie was now sitting behind the driver's seat, gun in position.

'Make it convincing,' Margaret hissed at Saint Cyr as he lowered the driver's side window. 'And don't get smart, or you're dead.'

'Visitors for Mr Haywood, Charlie,' Saint Cyr said to the uniformed attendant in the glass-fronted booth.

The man picked up a clipboard and examined it. 'Nothing here,' he said in a bored tone.

'That can't be right,' said Saint Cyr, a light sweat breaking out on his brow. 'Didn't Gina, his PA call down?'

The man shook his head. 'I'd better call up,' he said.

Margaret looked at Saint Cyr and bared her teeth, and Roxie dug the gun deeper into the upholstery, keeping it well out of the security man's sight.

A car drew up behind them. 'Come on Charlie,' said Saint Cyr. 'You're holding up the traffic. Soon as I get inside I'll get authorisation.'

'If you say so Mr Sincere,' said Charlie. 'But remember it's me who gets all the aggravation if people don't have the right clearance and I let them in.'

'I know. Just a glitch mate. Five minutes and I'll have it sorted.'

The car behind sounded its horn and Charlie looked over at it, a scowl on his face.

'*Charlie*,' said Saint Cyr. Then to Margaret. 'I told you we have strict rules about who comes and goes.'

'No problem. We're early anyway.' Then she smiled at Charlie through the open window. 'It is an important meeting. Short notice. You know how these things are.'

Charlie probably didn't, but his face softened and then hardened again as the car behind sounded its horn again. 'OK,' he said. 'But I want authorisation soon as.'

'No problem,' said Saint Cyr, as Charlie hit a button and the barrier rose.

'Thanks,' said Margaret and Saint Cyr in unison, and he let the car drift down the ramp towards the parking area.

75

———⟞⟐⟝———

'You did well there Peter,' said Margaret. 'Don't worry, this will be all over soon.'

'You're crazy. There's people with guns up there.'

'Yep, and there's people with guns down here,' smiled Roxie.

'The odds are against you.'

'Your sister isn't dead. Revenge is a hell of an incentive to win.'

'That's my spot,' he said, indicating a parking space marked AH No5.

'Spin the car round and reverse in,' Margaret ordered. 'Just in case we have to leave in a hurry. Be prepared, that's my motto.'

He did as he was told and the trio exited the car, leaving it unlocked and the keys in Margaret's pocket.

'Through here to the front,' he said, indicating a door.

'What's that?' asked Margaret, pointing at another, larger, accordion door.

'Service lift.'

'How high does it go?'

'Nineteenth. That's it.'

'Then I suppose you have to take the front lift, like we did the other day?'

'That's it.'

'And the front lift takes us right up to Haywood's office?'

'Right.'

'So if we use this one to the nineteenth, no one will know we're coming?' said Roxie, catching on to her sister's plan.

'There is CCTV down here.' He pointed at a camera above the door to the main part of the building.

'Who sees that?'

'An external security office. The company that owns the car park watched those cameras.'

'What about on your floors?'

'Our security office oversees that, and we can see the inside of the staff and visitors' lift.'

'But not this one? Right, we'll use this lift. Gives us an advantage.'

Saint Cyr tugged the lift door open. Inside was a scruffy metal box that smelled slightly of garbage. Saint Cyr pressed the button marked 19 and the lift ground slowly upwards.

'When we get there, I want to go up to Haywood's office.'

'You'll never make it.'

Margaret pulled the revolver from her pocket and Roxie again produced the big Colt. 'These say that we will,' said Margaret.

76

Eventually the lift stopped and Saint Cyr pulled the gate open. Inside was a large, scruffy loading bay with a key pad set to the side of another door in the opposite wall.

'Your card works on that,' said Margaret to Saint Cyr, at which he nodded.

'You're turning into such a good boy, Peter,' she said. 'It makes me think you have some surprises up your sleeve.'

He shrugged by way of reply. It was hard to do with a gun pressed hard into his spine.

'Now I'll tell you what we're going to do,' said Margaret. 'We're going to walk through like we all belong here. We don't want to use these.' She held up the gun then put her hand holding it into her handbag. 'But we will, if forced. You say there are armed men in here?'

He nodded.

'Christ! Peter, what kind of place is this? Thought you just dealt in import and export?'

He shrugged again. 'A place you don't want to be.'

'Quite the contrary. Now we go upstairs and see Mr Haywood.'

'OK. But you'll never get out alive.'

'Let's see about that.'

Saint Cyr used his keycard, punched in a series of numbers on the pad, then pushed open the exit door revealing an empty corridor. 'This way,' he said.

The two women followed him along the corridor, through another door and into the reception from the back. The same black girl as on her previous visit was at the desk – she looked shocked at their entrance.

'Good morning,' said Saint Cyr, sounding as if he was trying too hard to be natural.

'Good morning,' she replied, as he pushed through the double doors leading to the internal lift. When Margaret looked back, she was picking up the phone on her desk.

'We've been rumbled,' she said. 'Come on Peter, move.'

He took out his keycard again, inserted it in the slot by the side of the lift door, pressed four buttons and the lift door opened. He pressed for the penthouse office and the lift rose swiftly.

The door opened onto a small room where Haywood's PA sat behind a desk. 'Mr Saint Cyr,' she said, half rising from her seat. 'What's going on. Who are these people?'

'We're here to see Mr Haywood,' said Margaret.

'Impossible.'

Margaret pulled her gun out of her bag. 'I don't think so,' she said. 'I assume he's in.'

The PA watched open mouthed as the three of them

crossed her office and into Haywood's inner sanctum.
'I'm calling security,' she said.

'You do that,' said Margaret.

77

Haywood was sitting behind his desk, the sun shining through the window behind him, throwing his body into silhouette. 'What's this, St Cyr?' he said. 'Who are these unexpected, but charming visitors?'

'I'm sorry,' stuttered Saint Cyr. 'I had no choice. These bitches kidnapped me.'

'I told you about that Peter,' said Margaret, and smacked him on the back of the head with the barrel of her pistol.

'Maybe he likes being hurt,' said Roxie. 'He certainly asks for it enough.'

'Now I recognise you,' said Haywood to Margaret. 'The police officer – who wasn't one.'

'I am a police officer.'

'I know that too,' said Haywood. 'We had you on film. It wasn't hard making an identification.'

'Why didn't you do something about it?'

'Even police officers on suspension cause ripples if they disappear, or worse.'

'But not accountants and their secretaries?'

'Small fish,' said Haywood, dismissing her.

'You're incredibly arrogant Mr Haywood,' said Margaret. 'We're armed.'

'So are my security men. And I'm sure someone has alerted them by now. I trust Gina is not hurt.'

'The woman outside?' asked Roxie.

Haywood nodded.

'She's fine. We don't hurt women, unlike some people.'

'I'm not sure what you mean by that. Now ladies, this has all been very interesting, but I'm afraid you've had a wasted journey. I have nothing to say to you.'

'No Mr Haywood,' said Margaret. 'You're coming with us, and you are going to tell your story to another policeman.'

'You're so naive. And please, call me John,' smiled Haywood.

'You're enjoying this,' said Margaret, incredulously.

'Haven't had so much fun in years. Certainly livens up a dull Tuesday morning.'

'Up you get,' said Margaret, and that was when they heard the lift door in the outer office open.

78

'That'll be security now,' said Haywood. 'And I think there's someone you ought to meet. Peter, get the door will you.'

'Don't do it,' said Margaret. 'You'll leave it alone, if you know what's good for you.'

'I assure you it's important.'

Margaret moved to his side of the desk and stuck her pistol into his ear. 'OK, John,' she said. 'But if this goes pear-shaped, you'll be the first to get it.'

'So much aggression from such a pretty woman.'

'Shut up. All right Peter, get the door.'

He did as he was told, with Roxie's gun trained on him. Trent came through the door, arms raised away from his body. 'Got them boss,' he said. 'The woman's outside.'

'Good work Trent,' said Haywood.

'Easy,' he replied.

'Then bring her in, and let's get this over with.'

'Baxter,' said Trent through the open door. 'Come on.'

Another man entered the room, dragging Frankie with him. He had one of her arms twisted tightly behind her back, and in his other hand, close to her head, he held a 9mm Beretta automatic. She had tears running down her face, which was distorted with pain.

Margaret and Roxie looked stunned. 'What's she doing here?' said Margaret.

Through her tears Frankie said. 'It was my fault.'

'What was?' asked Roxie, bewildered.

'The money. I've got the money,' Frankie wailed.

'What?' Roxie again.

'The money Monty stole.'

'You?' said Roxie. 'How have you got it?'

'Sharon told me about it. She knew all along. She felt so guilty. That's why she did what she did.'

'Christ,' said Margaret, almost relaxing her grip on the gun in shock, a mixture of fear and surprise flitting across her face.

'I'm sorry to break up the family reunion,' interrupted Haywood, 'but this is hardly the time or place.'

'Did you know what she was going to do?' demanded Mags.

'Of course not,' said Frankie. 'But perhaps. I should've told you both. I just wanted the money for the children's sake. We could've gone away. A long way away from all this. Sharon as well. A fresh start.'

'If you're here, where are the kids?' said Roxie suddenly, turning on Haywood. 'If you've hurt them...' she snarled.

'The children are fine,' he replied. 'Just our little hostages to fortune. As soon as the money's back where it belongs, so will they be. Now, if you'll be kind enough to put your weapons on the floor, we'll try and sort this out with the minimum of fuss.'

79

'You reckon,' said Margaret. 'Well you're wrong. We're going to walk out of here, the three of us, and we'll go and get the kids. And you're coming with us. You and Peter.' She pushed her gun into the skin of Haywood's neck.

'I don't think so.'

Margaret smiled, lifted the gun she was holding and shot Trent in the thigh. His leg spouted blood and he cried out as much as in surprise as pain. Losing his grip on Frankie he fell to the floor. 'That's for our sister,' said Margaret. 'If it wasn't for you and this lot she'd still be alive, and so would Monty.'

The other man hauled his gun round, but Roxie fired too – and she was quicker. The heavy slug hit him in the upper body and he spun round and fell beside Trent. Frankie screamed and held her ears. 'Come on Frankie,' said Margaret. 'Keep it together.'

'Well, that's torn it,' said Roxie, her gun on Saint Cyr, who surveyed the scene, visibly shaking as Haywood rose up from his chair. 'Sit down,' ordered Margaret. 'I don't want to shoot you, but I will if necessary.

'My men,' said Haywood.

'As if you care. Plenty more where they came from.'

'That's what worries me,' said Roxie. 'So, where are Peter and Susan?' she asked Frankie.

'At that safe house. I went home to get them some things and there were men waiting. They made me take them to the house. That policeman was there.'

'Who?'

'Mahoney. He'd come over to relieve the policewoman, but it was no good. They hit him, and then brought me here. I told them I'd give them the money if they let us all go.'

'Mahoney,' said Margaret under her breath. 'Stupid.'

'So what now?' said Roxie.

'We leave, just as we planned all along,' said Mags.

'Hopeless,' said Haywood. 'You'll never make it.'

'We need a diversion,' said Margaret, and looked around, then out at the view from the penthouse. 'Got it. Give me your gun, Roxie. And get that one on the floor, and see if Mr Trent is armed. We need all the firepower we can get.'

Roxie did so, found another Beretta on Trent, and stuck both pistols into the pockets of her jacket.

'Right,' Margaret said to Haywood.'Get ready to go. Peter, you're coming too.'

Haywood shook his head and ducked as Margaret fired at the huge picture window behind his desk. One two, three shots, and the toughened glass began to splinter, then broke with a bang like a grenade going off, and the glass fell into shards down to the courtyard below. 'Hope no one's taking a smoke break,' she said, as a huge gust of air from outside came through the window frame, tearing at the clothes and hair of the people inside, picking up paper from Haywood's desk and thrusting it through the open door into the office beyond. Alarm bells began to ring through the building, and Margaret shouted to be heard above the din. 'Come on, let's get the hell out of here.'

80

Margaret and Roxie hustled Frankie, Haywood and Saint Cyr out of the office, past Haywood's open-mouthed PA who had been pushed against the inner wall by the force of the gale that was blowing through the room to the corridor, where the lift doors stood open. 'No point in trying to use the lift,' said Haywood. 'When the alarms went off, all lifts were locked.'

'No problem,' said Margaret. 'We'll take the stairs.'

'I can't hurry, I've got a heart condition,' he said.

'It'll be worse if I put a bullet in it. Just get moving.' The fire door opened easily, and they started downstairs where office workers were beginning to head down in packs. Inside the staircase the sound of the alarms were deafening. 'One word,' Margaret screamed in Haywood's ear, her gun jammed in his back. 'And I'll kill you.'

The journey down seemed to take an age, but eventually they arrived at the back of the building without being detected. The car park was beginning to fill up with staff from the building who were milling about. 'Get to the Lexus,' said Margaret above the din of the alarms. They ran across the car park, and piled into Saint Cyr's Lexus; Haywood, Saint Cyr and Roxie in the back, and Frankie in the front passenger seat. Margaret fired the car up and she sped towards the exit, hand on the horn, scattering pedestrians as they went.

The barrier was down and Charlie was blocking the road as an overhead metal gate began to descend. Margaret aimed the car at the ramp, the barrier smashed over the top of the car, Charlie dived for safety and the gate just caught the top of the Lexus with a screech of metal – but they were through. Margaret gunned the motor onto the main road, sideswiped a bendy bus, spun back onto the wrong side of the road narrowly missing a taxi, slammed her foot onto the accelerator and they were away.

'Nice driving,' said Roxie breathlessly. 'But I thought we were gonners there for a minute.'

'Trust me,' said Margaret as the car flew in the direction of the river. 'I'm a copper.'

'Or was,' said Haywood, before Roxie dug her gun into his ribs hard enough to break bone.

81

The drive to Guildford was uneventful, although Margaret was flashed by every speed camera on the way. 'There goes my licence if we get caught,' was all she said.

They took the back roads to the cottage where Margaret let the Lexus drift up to the turnaround. They could see Frankie and Mahoney's cars, parked close to the front gate. 'Right,' she said, reversing the car back out of sight up the drive, and forcing it back into the undergrowth. 'Frankie, you stay here. Haywood, Peter, you're with us.'

'Haywood, have you got a phone number for those people inside?' asked Margaret.

'Why would I? I don't deal with the help personally.'

'Peter?'

'They're Trent's men.'

'Jesus. It'll have to be Mahoney's phone then.' She took out her telephone and dialled Mahoney's number. Inside the cottage, they heard a ringing tone. After a minute the phone was answered. 'What?' said a gruff voice.

'Got your boss for you,' said Margaret, and handed the instrument to Haywood. 'Tell him who you are,' she said.

'You inside,' he said. 'My name is Roger Haywood. You know who I am?'

He seemed to get a positive answer.

'Tell him to show himself,' ordered Margaret.

Haywood did so.

The front door to the cottage opened and a man emerged. He was dressed in a track suit with a hooded top pulled up, a scarf covering the bottom of his face.

'Tell him to come to the gate,' said Margaret.

Haywood did so.

'Now tell him we're coming in.'

Once again Haywood obeyed.

Margaret and Roxie pushed the two men in front of them, forming a human shield and they all walked slowly up the gravel-topped drive towards the cottage.

Just as they drew level with the parked cars, Haywood suddenly pushed Saint Cyr out of the way, and dived between the vehicles shouting 'Shoot them. Shoot them,' at the hooded man who lifted his gun. But Margaret fired first and he took a bullet in the arm before running back into the cottage and slamming the door shut.

'Bastard,' said Roxie. 'I've had enough now,' and ran to where Haywood had vanished. He was lying on his back on the ground between the motors breathing heavily.

'The old jam tart?' said Roxie.

He could hardly speak, but fearing another trick, Roxie held the gun close to his head.

'I'm dying,' he gasped. 'Help me.'

'Like you helped all the people you've had murdered,' said Roxie. 'Fuck you.'

She slammed her hand on his chest – hard.

'Did that hurt?' she asked.

He nodded.

'Good,' she said. 'Serves you right,' and hit him again.

His eyes bulged, and he opened his mouth, but said nothing. He gasped once more, then he was still.

'Serves you right you old bastard,' said Roxie.

She crawled back to where Margaret and Saint Cyr were sheltered behind Mahoney's car. 'He's dead,' she said. 'Heart attack.'

'Looks like it's down to us now,' said Margaret.

'We could call the police.'

'Sure. So far we're guilty of kidnap, murder, criminal damage, not to mention car theft, leaving the scene of an accident and more speeding than you can shake a stick at. And probably half a dozen more crimes I can't even think of.'

'I get your point.'

'No. We'll sort this ourselves, and then vanish. Start again.'

'If we make it.'

'There's always that of course.'

'So what's the plan?' asked Roxie.

82

'Right Peter, what about you?' said Margaret.

'I could just go. Vanish myself,' he replied. 'Things can never be the same again with Haywood dead.'

'Understatement of the year,' said Margaret. 'No. I don't think so. Give me your hand.'

He did as he was told, and she cuffed it to the door handle of Mahoney's car. 'You stay here like a good boy,' she said. 'And we'll sort you out later. And keep your head down.'

He just pulled a face in disgust.

'Right,' said Margaret. 'It's all quiet in there, but there's one injured man, and according to Frankie two more. All armed. And then there's Peter and Susan. It's not looking good Roxie.'

'So what do we do?'

'If it wasn't for Mahoney and the kids I'd burn the fuckers out. As it is, they don't know we haven't called for backup, and are just waiting for SO19 to come steaming in guns blazing, so I reckon they'll make a move sharpish.'

'There's one thing,' said Roxie.

'What?'

'How did they get here? Sharon's car is here, and Mahoney's. But they must've driven themselves.'

'Stashed away on the woods like ours.'

'Right. And that's what they need.'

'Clever girl. That means they have to get out of there.'

As if to prove her point, one of the front windows broke with a crash, a gun barrel protruded and three shots were fired in rapid progression, hammering into the metal of Mahoney's car. Peter Saint Cyr, and the two women ducked down, as a figure emerged from behind the cottage, jumped the fence and vanished into the surrounding undergrowth.

'Told you,' said Margaret.

'What do we do?' asked Roxie.

'There's only two of them inside now. We go in and shoot the shit out of them.'

83

'You stay here,' Margaret said to Roxie. 'And give me some cover. I'm going round the back.'

'For Christ's sake, be careful.'

'I will.'

Carrying the two guns they'd picked up in Haywood's office, Margaret broke cover and headed for the back of the cottage. More shots rang out from the window and bullets dug up dirt around her feet as she ran, then Roxie fired a volley which dug dust from the bricks in the cottage wall, and the firing ceased.

Margaret threw herself into a forward roll and ended up by the fence that surrounded the cottage's small back garden. The hedge and rose bushes planted inside had been allowed to grow wild and gave her perfect cover, except for one narrow gap that led to a hole in the fence. At the back of the building was a glass-panelled door that she remembered led into the kitchen, one window on the ground floor, and two upstairs.

Betcha there's one of them up there, she thought. Well,

311

here goes nothing, and she stood. That window also blew out and more bullets smashed through the foliage in front of her. She pushed through the gap and ran for the back door. Christ, don't let there be anyone waiting there, she said to herself as she kicked the door open.

Inside the kitchen was empty.

She charged across the floor and saw Mahoney through the doorway, huddled on the sofa. He was bound with his own handcuffs, and next to him, with eyes like saucers, her niece and nephew. Then from the hall, the hooded man stuck his head round the door and Margaret let off a volley of bullets that drove him back out of sight. The small room was filled with smoke and her ears rang with the noise of the shots. 'Get down,' she screamed at Mahoney. 'Get the kids down on the floor.'

He reacted with speed, and although his wrists were tied together he wrestled the children to the floor, then lay over them, his body protecting them.

Margaret saw his eyes on her, and she smiled, then heard footsteps from the floor above. The cottage was old and the ceiling in the kitchen was plaster – so she bet that the floor above was wooden. Mags fired through the ceiling and heard a scream of pain and a heavy thump and plaster gently fell around her like snow.

She looked back into the living room. All was quiet for a moment, so she dropped to the floor and crawled over to Mahoney and the children. She pulled the keys to her cuffs from her pocket and miraculously they fitted Mahoney's. He threw them aside and she thrust one of her guns into his hand. 'I hope you can use this,' she said.

'Where did you spring from?' he asked.

'No time. There's one outside.'

He nodded, as they heard the front door open only to be answered with more shots from Roxie's gun, then the door slammed again. Margaret made for the hall door and peered round to see the hoodie facing her, his gun arm raised. He fired and she fired back, knocking him to the floor. The silence was broken by the sound of a gun being cocked up the short flight of stairs. Mahoney appeared behind her, fired, and the gun bounced down the flight – followed by a body.

'Thanks Mahoney,' she said. 'Looks like we had a result.'

84

But she spoke too soon as they heard the sound of a heavy engine outside, and a man's voice shouted to Roxie to drop her weapon. 'What now?' said Margaret, going to the window but keeping well out of sight.

Outside, she saw a Land Rover parked next to Mahoney and Frankie's cars. A man she'd never seen before was outside holding Frankie tightly with a gun pressed to her head.

'Christ,' she said, feeling the familiar irritation. 'Can't that bloody sister of mine do anything right.'

'You inside,' shouted the man. 'Come out, hands raised. All of you. The children too.'

'Come on,' said Margaret to Mahoney. 'Do as he says.'

The four left the house and walked down the path.

'Where's the rest?' demanded the man. 'My mates.'

'Didn't make it,' said Margaret.

'Who the fuck are you?' said the man.

'My sisters,' said Frankie.

'A couple of birds, I don't believe this. So what's stop-ping me killing all of you?'

Suddenly Saint Cyr jumped up from the side of Mahoney's car. 'Don't shoot her,' he yelled. 'She's got the…'

The armed man turned his gun on him, and as he did so, Roxie pulled the .38 from the back of her jeans and, just like she'd done in Spain to Tony, shot him on the eye.

He dropped like a stone, but as he did so he pulled the trigger of his gun, the bullet flying off to take Saint Cyr in the chest.

The tableau was silent for a moment, then Frankie said, her voice wavering, 'Thank you Roxie. You saved my life.'

'That's what sisters are for,' Roxie replied, then turned to Margaret. 'So what now?' she asked,

'I could call the station,' said Mahoney. 'I know what happened.'

'But there's more,' said Margaret. 'Much more.'

'I've got the money,' interrupted Frankie. 'We could just vanish.'

'Not a bad idea,' said Margaret. 'Take that Range Rover and get to France.'

'Then Spain,' said Frankie.

'Actually,' said Roxie. 'I don't think Spain is such a good idea.'

'If you're going I'm going with you,' said Mahoney to Margaret.

'It's love,' said Roxie. 'I knew it.'

'You're a sweet bloke Mahoney,' said Margaret. 'But I don't know.'

They all stood amongst the carnage, until Margaret said. 'Well everybody, let's make up our minds. What's it to be?'